KU-411-655

COLETTE

Claudine in Paris

TRANSLATED FROM THE FRENCH BY
Antonia White

VINTAGE

14

Vintage
20 Vauxhall Bridge Road,
London SW1V 2SA

Vintage Classics is part of the Penguin Random House
group of companies whose addresses can be found
at global.penguinrandomhouse.com.

Penguin
Random House
UK

Copyright © Martin Secker & Warburg Ltd 1958

First published in France as *Claudine à Paris,* attributed
to Willy, in 1901
This translation first published in Great Britain by
Martin Secker & Warburg in 1958
First published by Vintage Classics in 2001

www.vintage-books.co.uk

A CIP catalogue record for this book is available from the British Library

ISBN 9780099422525

Printed and bound in Great Britain by Clays Ltd, Elcograf S.p.A.

Penguin Random House is committed to a sustainable future for
our business, our readers and our planet. This book is made
from Forest Stewardship Council® certified paper.

MIX
Paper from
responsible sources
FSC
www.fsc.org   FSC® C018179

COLETTE

Colette, the creator of Claudine, Cheri and Gigi, and one of France's outstanding writers, had a long, varied and active life. She was born in Burgundy in 1873 into a home overflowing with dogs, cats and children, and educated at the local village school. At the age of twenty she moved to Paris with her first husband, the notorious writer and critic Henry Gauthiers-Viller (Willy). By locking her in her room, Willy forced Colette to write her first novels (the *Claudine* sequence), which he published under his name. They were an instant success. Colette left Willy in 1906 and worked in music halls as an actor and dancer. She had a love affair with Napoleon's niece, married twice more, and had a baby at 40 and at 47. Her writing, which included novels, portraits, essays and a large body of autobiographical prose, was admired by Proust and Gide. She was the first woman President of the Académie Goncourt, and when she died, aged 81, she was given a state funeral and buried in Père Lachaise Cemetery in Paris.

ALSO BY COLETTE

Fiction

Claudine at School
Claudine Married
Claudine and Annie
Gigi
The Cat
Chéri
The Last of Chéri
Chance Acquaintances
Julie de Carneilhan
The Ripening Seed
The Vagabond
Break of Day
The Innocent Libertine
Mitsou
The Other One
The Shackle

Non-fiction

My Apprenticeships and *Music-Hall Sidelights*
The Blue Lantern
My Mother's House and *Sido*
The Pure and the Impure

PREFACE

I have told in *Mes Apprentissages* how, some two years after our marriage, therefore about 1895, Monsieur Willy said to me one day:

'You ought to jot down on paper some memories of the Primary School. I might be able to make something out of them . . . Don't be afraid of racy details.'

This curious and still comparatively unknown man, who put his name to I know not how many volumes without having written a single one of them, was constantly on the look-out for new talents for his literary factory. It was not in the least surprising that he should have extended his investigations as far as his own home.

'I was recovering from a long and serious illness which had left my mind and body lazy. But, having found at a stationer's some exercise-books like the ones I had at school, and bought them again, their cream-laid pages, ruled in grey, with red margins, their black linen spines, and their covers bearing a medallion and an ornate title *Le Calligraphe* gave my fingers back a kind of itch for doing "lines", for the passivity of a set task. A certain watermark, seen through the cream-laid paper, made me feel six years younger. On a stub of a desk, the window behind me, one shoulder askew and my knees crossed, I wrote with application and indifference . . .

'When I had finished, I handed over to my husband a closely-written manuscript which respected the margins. He skimmed through it and said:

'"I made a mistake, this can't be of the slightest use . . ."

'Released, I went back to the sofa, to the cat, to books, to silence, to a life that I tried to make pleasant for myself and that I did not know was unhealthy for me.

'The exercise-books remained for two years at the bottom of a drawer. One day Willy decided to tidy up the contents of his desk.

'The appalling counter-like object of sham ebony with a crimson baize top displayed its deal drawers and disgorged bundles of old papers and once again we saw the forgotten exercise-books in which I had scribbled: *Claudine à l'école*.

'"Fancy," said Monsieur Willy. "I thought I had put them in the waste-paper basket."

'He opened one exercise-book and turned over the pages:
'"It's charming . . ."

'He opened a second exercise-book, and said no more – a third, then a fourth . . .

'"Good Lord," he muttered, "I'm an utter imbecile . . ."

'He swept up the exercise-books haphazard, pounced on his flat-brimmed hat and rushed off to a publisher . . . And that was how I became a writer.'

But that was also how I very nearly missed ever becoming a writer. I lacked the literary vocation and it is probable that I should never have produced another line if, after the success of *Claudine à l'école*, other imposed tasks had not, little by little, got me into the habit of writing.

Claudine à l'école appeared in 1900, published by Paul Ollendorff, bearing Willy's sole name as the author. In the interval, I had to get back to the job again to put a little 'spice' into my text.

'Couldn't you,' Willy said to me, 'hot this – these childish reminiscences up a little? For example, a too passionate friendship between Claudine and one of her schoolmates . . . And then some dialect, lots of dialect words . . . Some naughty pranks . . . You see what I mean?'

The pliancy of extreme youth is only equalled by its lack of scruples. What was the extent of Willy's collaboration? The manuscripts furnish a partial answer to a question that has been asked a hundred times. Out of the four *Claudine* books, only the manuscripts of *Claudine en ménage* and *Claudine s'en va* have been saved from the destruction which Willy ordered Paul Barlet to carry out. Paul Barlet, known as Paul Héon – secretary, friend, Negro and extremely honourable man – suspended the execution, which had begun to be carried out, and brought me what remained, which I still possess.

Turning over the pages of those exercise-books is not without interest. Written entirely in my handwriting, a very fine writing appears at distant intervals, changing a word, adding a pun or a very sharp rebuke. Likewise one could also read (in *Claudine en ménage* and *Claudine s'en va*) two more important re-written passages pasted over the original which I am omitting in the present edition.

The success of the *Claudine* books was, for the period, very great. It inspired fashions, plays, and beauty-products. Being honourable, and above all indifferent, I kept silent about the truth, which did not become known till very much later. Nevertheless, it is today for the first time that the *Claudine* books appear under the single name of their single author. I should also be glad if, henceforth, *La Retraite sentimentale* – a pretty title suggested by Alfred Vallette – were considered as the last book in the *Claudine* series. The reader will find this far more satisfactory from the point of view of both logic and convenience.

COLETTE

ONE

TODAY, ONCE AGAIN, I am beginning to keep my diary. It was forcibly interrupted during my illness – my serious illness. For I really believe I've been very ill indeed!

I still don't feel any too strong even now, but the time when I had high fever and was in such utter despair seems a long time ago. Of course I can't conceive that people live in Paris for pleasure, of their own free will, but I do begin to understand that one can get interested in what goes on inside these huge six-storeyed boxes.

For the honour of my notebooks, I shall have to explain why I come to be in Paris; why I've left Montigny, that beloved, quiet fantastic school where Mademoiselle Sergent, oblivious of Mrs Grundy's comments, continues to cherish her little Aimée while the pupils kick up a hullabaloo; why Papa has deserted his slugs and so on. Oh dear, there's so much to tell . . . I shall be awfully tired by the time I've finished! Because, you know, I'm thinner than I was last year and a little taller too. In spite of having turned seventeen the day before yesterday, I barely look sixteen – let me look at myself in the glass. Yes . . . no doubt about it

Pointed chin, you're attractive but don't, I implore you, overdo that point. Hazel eyes, you persist in being hazel and I can't blame you for it; but don't retreat under my eyebrows with that excessive modesty. Mouth, you're still my mouth, but pale that I can't resist rubbing those short, colourless lips with petals pulled from the red geranium in the window. (Incidentally it only gives them a horrid, purplish tinge that I

1

promptly lick off.) As to you, my poor little white, anaemic ears, I hide you under my curly hair and secretly look at you from time to time and pinch you to make you redden. But it's my hair that's the worst of all. I can't touch it without wanting to cry . . . They've cut them all off, just below the ear – my auburn ringlets, my lovely, smoothly rolled ringlets! To be sure, the ten centimetres that remain to me are doing their utmost; they curl and fluff out and are growing as fast as ever they can. But I'm so miserable every morning when I involuntarily make the gesture of lifting up my mane before soaping my neck.

Papa, with that magnificent beard of yours, I'm nearly as furious with you as I am with myself. You simply can't imagine a father like mine! Just you listen.

When his great treatise on the *Malacology of Fresnois* was nearly finished, Papa sent a large portion of his manuscript to Masson, a publisher in Paris. From that day on, he was devoured by an appalling fever of impatience. What! His galleys corrected and sent off to the Boulevard Saint-Germain in the morning (eight hours' journey by rail) had not arrived back at Montigny that self-same night? Ah! Doussine the postman heard some home truths. 'Filthy Bonapartist of a postman, not bringing me my proofs! He's a cuckold, it serves him right!' And the compositors . . . my goodness me! Threats of scalping these perpetrators of scandalous printer's errors and anathemas against these 'vermin of Sodom' were boomed out all day long. Fanchette, my beautiful cat, who is a very correct person, raised indignant eyebrows. November was rainy and the neglected slugs died one after the other. So much so, that, one evening, Papa, with one hand in his tri-coloured beard, declared to me: 'My book isn't getting on at all, the printers don't give a damn for me. The most reasonable (*sic*) thing to do would be for us to go and live in Paris.' This proposal completely bowled me over. Such simplicity, combined with such utter craziness, excited me, and all I asked was a week to think it over. 'Be quick about it,' said Papa, 'I've got someone for our house. What's-his-name wants to rent it.' Oh the duplicity of the most guileless fathers! This one had already arranged everything behind my back and I had had no inkling of this threatened departure!

Two days later, at school, where, on Mademoiselle's advice, I was vaguely thinking of working for my Higher Certificate, the gawk Anaïs was even more shrewish than usual. I couldn't stand any more of it so I said, with a shrug, 'Come off it, old thing. Anyway, you won't be able to bore me stiff much longer. In a month's time, I'm going to live in Paris.' The stupefaction she hadn't time to hide absolutely delighted me. She rushed up to Luce: 'Luce! You're going to lose your great friend! My dear, you'll weep tears of blood when Claudine goes off to Paris! Hurry up, cut off a lock of your hair, exchange your last vows of eternal friendship: you've only just time!' Luce was petrified. She spread out her fingers like palm-leaves, opened her green, lazy eyes to their fullest extent, and shamelessly burst into loud tears. She got on my nerves. 'Yes, I really am going. And I shan't be the least bit sorry to see the last of the whole lot of you!'

At home, having made up my mind, I gave Papa my solemn 'Yes'. He combed his beard complacently and announced:

'Pradeyron is already hunting for a flat for us. Where? I haven't the least idea. Provided I've room for my books, I don't care a damn about the neighbourhood. What about you?

'I don't care a . . . I mean, I don't mind either.'

In reality, I knew nothing whatever about it. How could you expect a Claudine who had never left the big house and the beloved garden of Montigny to know what she wanted in Paris and which neighbourhood to choose? Fanchette knew nothing about it either. But I became agitated and, as in all the great crises of my life, I took to wandering about while Papa, suddenly practical – no, that's going too far – suddenly *active*, flung himself tempestuously into the business of packing.

For a hundred reasons, I preferred to escape to the woods and not to have to listen to Mélie's furious lamentations.

Mélie is fair, lazy, and faded. She was once extremely pretty. She does the cooking, brings me water, and pilfers fruit from our garden to give it to vague 'acquaintances'. But Papa assured me that, when I was a baby, she nourished me with

'superb' milk, and that she is still devoted to me. She sings a
great deal and knows by heart a varied repertory of broad,
not to say obscene, songs of which I remember quite a
number. (And they say I don't cultivate the social graces!)
There's a very pretty one:

> He drank five or six straight off
> And never stopped for breath
> Tra la la . . .
> Just to show he liked the stuff
> He near drank himself to death
> Tra la la . . . , etc., etc.

Mélie tenderly cherishes my defects as well as my virtues.
She declares enthusiastically that I'm 'ever so fetching', that I
have 'a lovely body', and concludes: 'It's a pity you haven't
got a young man.' Mélie includes the whole of nature in her
innocent and disinterested urge to excite and appease the
desires of the flesh. In the spring, when Fanchette miaows and
purrs and rolls on her back in the garden paths, Mélie
obligingly summons the tom-cats and attracts them with
platefuls of raw meat. Then she sentimentally contemplates
the resulting idylls. Standing in the garden, in a dirty apron,
she lets the rump of veal or the jugged hare 'catch', as she
dreamily cups her uncorseted breasts in the palms of her
hands as if she were weighing them – a frequent gesture of
hers that always manages to irritate me. In spite of myself, I
feel vaguely disgusted to think that I was suckled at them.

All the same, if I were just a silly little fool and not a very
sensible girl, Mélie would obligingly do everything necessary
to help me lapse from virtue. But I only laugh at her when she
mentions the subject of a lover . . . *no*, thank you very much!
. . . and I give her a push and say: 'Go and tell that stuff to
Anaïs, you'll get a better reception from *her*.'

Mélie swore on her mother's blood that she wouldn't come
to Paris. I told her: 'I don't give a damn whether you come or
not.' So then she began to make her preparations, prophesy-
ing a thousand appalling catastrophes as she did so.

*

As for me, I wandered along the slushy paths in the rusty woods that smelt of mushrooms and wet moss, gathering the yellow chanterelles that go so well with creamy sauces and casserole of veal. And, little by little, I realized that this move to Paris was sheer madness. Perhaps, if I implored Papa or better still bullied him? But what would Anaïs say? And Luce, who might think I was staying because of her? No. Hang it all! I needn't do anything about it unless Paris turned out to be too intolerable.

One day, in the clearing of the Valley Wood as I was looking down at the woods, the woods that I love better than anything in the whole world, and up at the Saracen tower that gets lower every year, I saw so clearly and sharply the folly, the misery of going away that I nearly raced down the hill and back to the house to implore them, to *order* them to undo the packing cases and unwrap the legs of the chairs.

Why didn't I do it? Why did I stay up there, with my mind a blank and my hands icy under my red hooded cloak? The chestnuts, in their husks, fell on me and pricked my head a little, like balls of wool with darning-needles left stuck in them.

I'm skipping a good deal. Farewells at school; a chilly good-bye to the Headmistress (amazing Mademoiselle! With her little Aimée glued to her, she said 'au revoir' as if I were coming back that same evening); a mocking farewell from Anaïs: 'I don't wish you good luck, old dear. Luck follows you everywhere. No doubt you won't deign to write to me except to announce your wedding'; anguished and tearful farewells from Luce who has confected a little purse for me in yellow and black embroidery silk and exquisitely bad taste. She has also presented me with a lock of her hair in a fancy-wood needle-case. She has 'empicated' these souvenirs so that I shall never lose them.

(For those who do not know about the witching spell of 'empication', the process is as follows: you place the object O, to be empicated, on the ground; you enclose it between two brackets whose joined ends (XO) cross over each other and inside which you inscribe X on the left of the object. After that, you can set your mind at rest; the empication is infallible. One can also spit on the object but this is not absolutely indispensable.)

Poor Luce said to me: 'Go on, you don't believe I'll be miserable. But you just wait and see what lengths I'm ready to go to. You know, I'm absolutely fed up with my sister and Mademoiselle. There was no one but *you* here, the only thing that kept me going was you. You wait and see!' I gave the heartbroken creature a great many kisses, on her resilient cheeks and her wet eyelashes and the brown and white nape of her neck; I kissed her dimples and her irregular, too short little nose. She had never had so many caresses from me and the poor child's despair redoubled. Perhaps, for one year, I might have made her very happy. (It wouldn't have cost you as much as all that, Claudine, I know you!) But I don't regret in the least not having done so.

The physical horror or seeing the furniture moved and my little possessions packed up made me shivery and cross, like a cat in the rain. Having to watch the departure of my little ink-stained mahogany desk and my narrow walnut four-poster bed and the old Norman sideboard that serves me as a linen cupboard nearly threw me into hysterics. Papa, more insufferably pleased with himself than every, paraded about the scene of disaster, singing: '*The English full of arrogance, Came to set siege to Lorient. And the men of Lower Brittany* . . . ' (unfortunately, one cannot quote the rest). I've never detested him so much as I did that day.

At the last moment, I thought I had lost Fanchette. Just as horrified as I was she had fled wildly into the garden and taken refuge in the coal-shed. I had endless trouble recapturing her and shutting her up in a travelling-basket. She was spitting, black all over, and swearing like a fiend. When it comes to baskets, the only one she approves of is the meat-basket.

Two

THE JOURNEY, THE arrival, and the first days of settling-in are all confused in a general fog of misery. The dark flat, between two courtyards in this dismal, shabby Rue Jacob, reduced me to a broken-hearted stupor. I stood without moving, watching the crates of books arrive one by one, then the uprooted furniture; I watched Papa, bustling and excited, nailing up shelves, pushing his desk from corner to corner, rejoicing out loud at the flat's situation: 'Two steps from the Sorbonne, just by the Geographical Society, and the Sainte-Geneviève Library only a stone's throw away!' I heard Mélie moaning over the smallness of her kitchen . . . which is on the other side of the landing and actually one of the best rooms in the flat . . . and I suffered because she served us, on the excuse of the moving-in being unfinished and difficult, with stuff to eat that was . . . unfinished and difficult to digest. I was obsessed with one single idea: 'Is it really *me* here, was it really *me* who let this crazy thing happen?' I refused to go out; I obstinately refused to do anything useful; I wandered from one room to another, with a lump in my throat and no appetite whatsoever. By the end of ten days, I looked so queer that Papa himself noticed it and was promptly seized with panic, for he goes to extremes in everything and is nothing if not thorough. He sat me on his knees, against his great tri-coloured beard, and rocked me between his gnarled hands that smelt of fir from putting up so many shelves . . . I said nothing; I gritted my teeth because I still felt a savage resentment against him . . . And then, my taut nerves gave way in a tremendous burst of hysteria and Mélie put me to bed, burning hot all over.

After that, a very long time went by. Something like brain-fever, with symptoms of typhoid. I do not think I was very delirious, but I fell into a woeful darkness and I was aware of nothing but my head which ached so dreadfully! I can remember lying for hours on my left side, tracing the outlines of the fantastic fruits printed on my bed-curtains with the tip of my finger. The fruit is a kind of apple with eyes in it. Even now, I have only to look at it to drift off at once into a world of nightmares and dizzy dreams where everything is all mixed up: Mademoiselle, and Aimée, and Luce, a wall that's just going to collapse on me, the spiteful Anaïs, and Fanchette who becomes as big as a donkey and sits on my chest. I can remember, too, Papa bending over me; his beard and his face looked enormous as I pushed him away with my two feeble arms, then pulled my hands back at once because the cloth of his overcoat seemed so harsh and so painful to touch! Last of all, I remember a gentle doctor, a little fair man with a woman's voice and cold hands that made me shudder all over.

For two months, they couldn't comb my hair, and, as my matted curls hurt me when I rolled my head on my pillow, Mélie cut them off with her scissors, quite close to my head. She had to manage as best she could and the result was uneven layers like doorsteps! Heavens, what luck that gawk Anaïs can't see me like this, transformed into a boy! She was jealous of my chestnut curls and used to pull them slyly during recreation.

Little by little, my taste for life returned. I noticed one morning, when they had been able to sit me up in bed, that the rising sun came into my room and that the striped red and white paper livened up the walls, and my thoughts began to run on fried potatoes.

'Mélie, I'm hungry. Mélie, what's that smell coming from your kitchen? Mélie, my little looking-glass! Mélie, some eau-de-Cologne to wash my ears with! Mélie, what can one see out of the window? I want to get up.'

'Oh, my little pet, aren't you getting *aggravating* again? It's because you're better. But you wouldn't be able so much as to stand up on your two feet and the doctor's said you're not to.'

'He has, has he? Wait . . . get back . . . don't move! You just see!'

Hop! In spite of the agonized remonstrances and the cries of: 'Sakes alive! You'll fall flat on your face, my precious girlie, I'll tell the doctor!' I made a tremendous effort and managed to drag my legs out of bed . . . Alack! What had they done with my calves? And my knees, how enormous they looked! Gloomily, I got back into bed, already too exhausted to make any more effort.

I've consented to stay fairly good, though I find that 'fresh eggs' in Paris have a peculiar taste of printed paper. It's nice in my room: there's a wood fire in it and I like looking at the red and white striped wallpaper (I've said that already), at my double-doored Norman sideboard that contains my small wardrobe of clothes and lingerie; its top is worn and chipped, I've scratched it a bit and spilt some ink on it. It stands against the longest wall of my rectangular room, next to my bed, my walnut four-poster with its chintz curtains (we're out of date) patterned with red and yellow flowers and fruits on a white ground. Opposite my bed, my little old-fashioned mahogany desk. No carpet; by way of a bedside rug, a big white poodle-skin. A tub armchair in tapestry, a little threadbare on the arms. A low chair made of old wood, with a red and yellow straw seat. Another, just as low, enamelled white. And a little square cane table, varnished its natural colour. What a jumble! But the general effect has always seemed exquisite to me. My dressing-table is a Louis XV console with a pink marble top. (It's sheer waste, it's imbecility: it would be infinitely better in its right place in the drawing-room. I know that perfectly well but I'm not Papa's daughter for nothing). Let us complete the inventory: a big commonplace wash-basin, an impetuous water-jug and, no, *not* a hip-bath. Instead of a hip-bath that freezes your feet and makes ridiculous noises like stage-thunder, a wooden tub, *actually* a 'a small wine-vat'! A Good Montigny wine-vat, of copper-hooped beech, that I squat in, tailor-fashion, and that rasps the behind pleasantly as one sits in the hot water.

So I meekly eat eggs and, as I'm absolutely forbidden to read, I only read a little (my head begins to swim at once). I can't managed to explain how the joy of waking up gradually clouds over as the day wanes till I'm reduced to melancholy and to curling myself up into an unsociable ball, in spite of Fanchette's attempts to rouse me.

Fanchette, lucky girl, has taken her internment gaily. She has accepted, without protest, a tray of sawdust, hidden in the space beside my bed, in which to deposit her little messes. Leaning over her, I amuse myself by following the phases of an important operations in the expression of her cat's features. Fanchette washes her hind paws carefully, between the toes. Her face is discreet and says nothing. An abrupt pause in the washing: her face is serious, slightly anxious. A sudden change of pose; she sits down on her behind. Her eyes are cold, rather severe. She gets up, takes three steps, and sits down again. Then, irrevocable decision, she jumps off the bed, runs to her tray, scratches . . . and there is nothing at all. The indifferent expression returns. But not for long. Her anxious eyebrows draw together: feverishly, she scratches the sawdust again, tramples it down, looks for a good place and, for three minutes, seems lost in bitter thoughts, her eyes fixed and starting out of their sockets. For she is, deliberately, slightly constipated. At last, she slowly gets up and, with minute pre-cautions, covers up the corpse, wearing the earnest expression suitable to this funeral operation. A little supererogatory scratching *round* the tray, then she goes straight into a loose-limbed, diabolic caper, prelude to a goat-like skipping and leaping, the dance of liberation. At that, I laugh and call out: 'Mélie, quick! Come and change the cat's tray!'

I've begun to get interested in the noises in the courtyard. A big, depressing courtyard; at the far end of it, the backside of a black house. In the courtyard itself, anonymous little buildings with tiled roofs . . . tiles like the ones you see in the country. A low dark door opens, I'm told, on the Rue Visconti. I've never seen anyone walking across this courtyard but workmen in blouses and sad, bare-headed women whose busts sag down towards their hips at every step in the way peculiar to worn-out drudges. A child plays there silently, invariably all by himself. I think he belongs to the concierge of this sinister block of flats. On the ground floor of our home – if I dare call it 'home', this square house full of people whom I don't know and instinctively dislike – a dirty servant-girl in a Breton coif punishes a poor little dog every morning. No doubt it misbehaves during the night in the kitchen, but oh how it yelps and it cries! Let that girl just wait till I'm well, she shall perish by my hand and no other! Lastly, every Thursday, a barrel-organ grinds out shocking love-songs from ten to eleven, and every Friday a pauper (they say a pauper here and not 'an unfortunate' as they do in Montigny), a real classic pauper with a white beard comes and declaims pathetically: 'Ladies and gentlemen . . . remember . . . a pore unfortunate! . . . Can't hardly see at all! . . . He looks to your kind 'eartedness! . . . Ladies and gentlemen, please! (one, two, three . . .) . . . *if* you p-p-please!' All this in a little minor sing-song that ends up in the major. I make Mélie throw this venerable old man four sous out of the window; she grumbles and says that I spoil beggars.

Papa, freed from anxiety and radiant in the knowledge that I'm really and truly getting better, takes advantage of this by no longer appearing at home except at meal times. Oh the Libraries and the Public Records Offices – the Nationale, the Cardinale and all the rest – that he tramps through, dusty and bearded and looking like one of the Bourbons!

Poor Papa, didn't he nearly start it all up again on February morning by bringing me a bunch of violets? The smell of the living flowers, their cool touch, suddenly ripped back the curtain of forgetfulness that my fever had stretched over the Montigny I had left . . . Once again I saw the transparent, leafless woods, the roads edged with shrivelled blue sloes and frost-bitten hips, and the village built in tiers, and the tower with the dark ivy – the only thing that remained green – and the white School in the mild, unglittering sunshine. I smelt the musky, rotten smell of the dead leaves; I smelt, too, the vitiated atmosphere of ink and paper and web sabots in the

11

classroom. And Papa, frantically clutching his Louis XIV nose, and Mélie, anxiously fiddling with her breasts, thought I was going to be seriously ill again. The gentle doctor with the feminine voice came rushing up the three flights of stairs and assured them that it was nothing at all.

(I detest that fair man with the light spectacles. I admit that he looks after me well, but, at the sight of him, I put my hands under the sheets, I curl up like a gun-dog and I clench my toes, as Fanchette does when I want to see her claws close to. This feeling is completely unjust but I haven't the least intention of overcoming it. I don't like a man whom I don't know touching me and fingering me and laying his head on my chest to hear if I'm breathing properly. Besides, hang it all, he might at least warm his hands!)

It *was* nothing at all and, actually, I was soon able to get up. And, from that day, my preoccupations took another turn.

'Mélie, whoever's going to make my dresses now?'

'Haven't the faintest idea, my lamby. Why don't you ask Ma'ame Coeur to give you an address?'

Why, Mélie was absolutely right!

Really, it was dense not to have thought of that before, because, good gracious, 'Ma'ame Coeur' isn't a distant relative, she's Papa's sister. But this admirable father of mine has always managed, with perfect ease, to keep free of any kind of family ties and duties. I really believe I've only seen her once in my life, Aunt Coeur. I was nine and Papa brought me to Paris with him. She looked like the Empress Eugénie; I think that was to annoy her brother who looks, himself, like Louis XIV. Quite a royal family! She's a widow, this amiable woman, and, as far as I know, has no children.

Each day, I wander a little further through the flat. I'm so thin that I'm quite lost in my flowing dressing-gown of faded purple velveteen, gathered on the shoulders. In the gloomy dressing-room, Papa has installed the furniture from his smoking-room and from the drawing-room at Montigny.

It hurts me to see little low, wide, slightly ripped Louis XVI armchairs side by side with the two Arab tables, the Moorish armchair of inlaid wood and the divan covered with an

12

oriental carpet. Claudine, you'll have to do something about that . . .

I finger the knick-knacks, I pull out a Moroccan stool, I put the little sacred cow back on the chimneypiece (it's a very old Japanese curio, twice stuck together again, thanks to Mélie), then, all at once, I plump down on the divan, against the glass where my eyes, so much too big, and my hollow cheeks and most, most of all my poor hair in those uneven layers, throw me into black depression. Well, old thing, suppose this moment you had to climb the big walnut-tree in the garden at Montigny? Where's your wonderful nimbleness, where are your agile legs and your monkey's hands that made such a brisk *slap* on the branches when you used to be up at the top in ten seconds? You look like a little girl of fourteen who's been martyred.

One night at the dinner-table, as I nibbled – without seeming to – some bread crusts that are still strictly forbidden, I questioned the author of the *Malacology of Fresnois*.

'Why haven't we seen my aunt yet? Haven't you written to her? Haven't you been to see her?'

Papa, with the condescension one displays to mad people, asked me gently, with a clear eye and a soothing voice:

"Which aunt, darling?'

Accustomed to his frank absent-mindedness, I made him grasp that I was talking about his sister.

Thereupon he exclaimed, full of admiration:

'You think of everything! Ten thousand herds of swine! Dear old girl, how please she'll be to know we're in Paris.' He added, his face clouding: 'She'll hook on to me like a damn' leech.'

Little by little, I extended my walks as far as the book-lair. Papa has put up shelves all round the three walls of the room that gets the daylight from a big window (the only even moderately light room in the flat is the kitchen – though Mélie picturesquely insists that 'you can't see in it neither with your head or your tail'), and, in the middle, he has planted his thuya-wood and brass desk, furnished with castors, that rambles into all the corners, laboriously followed by an old low-seated, high-backed armchair of red leather that's gone white at the corners and is split on both arms. The little wheeled ladder to reach the high-perched dictionaries, a trestle-table – and that's all.

Now that I'm getting stronger every day, I come and cheer myself up with the well-known titles of the books and now and then I re-open the Balzac (in Bertall's shocking edition) or Voltaire's *Dictionnaire philosophique*. What am I doing with this dictionary? Boring myself . . . and learning various undesirable things, nearly always shocking ones (undesirable things are not always shocking; on the contrary). But, ever since I've learnt to read, I've been 'Papa's bookworm' and, though I'm not in the least shocked, I don't get over-excited either.

I have explored Pap's 'sanctum'. That Papa of mine! In his bedroom, hung with a wallpaper strewn with bunches of rustic flowers – a young girl's wallpaper – he had a four-poster too, with its mattress sloped at a vertiginous angle – Papa will only sleep in a sitting position. I will spare you the Empire furniture, the big wicker armchairs cushioned with brochures and scientific reviews, the coloured planks hung all over the place, strewn with slugs, millipedes, and various horrid little creatures! On the chimneypiece, rows of fossils that were molluscs a good long time ago. And, on the floor beside the bed, two ammonites as big as cartwheels! Long live Malacology! Our home is the sanctuary of a noble – and I dare to say unsullied – Science.

The dining-room isn't interesting. If the sideboard weren't Burgundian and the big chairs Burgundian too, I'd find it very commonplace. The too-rustic dresser no longer has the dark panelling at Montigny as a background. Having nowhere else to put it, Mélie has planked down the big linen-cupboard there. It's beautiful, with its Louis XV panels adorned with musical emblems, but like everything else, it is sad and exiled. It thinks of Montigny, as I do.

When the doctor I dislike told me, with an air of modest triumph, that I could go out, I exclaimed: 'Nothing would induce me to!' I said it with such splendid indignation that it left him – it's the only word – stupid.

'Why?'

'Because my hair's been cut off! I won't go out till I've got long hair.'

'Very well, my child, then you'll get ill again. You need, you absolutely must have fresh air.'

'You make me sick. What I absolutely must have is *hair*.

He went away, mild as ever. Why didn't he get angry? I'd have said some hard things to him to relieve my feelings . . .

Feeling thoroughly embittered, I studied myself in looking-glasses. I decided that it wasn't so much the shortness of my hair as its unevenness that made me look more than ever like a melancholy cat. The desk scissors to the rescue! They were too big and blunt. My work-box ones? They were too short. Of course there were Mélie's scissors . . . but she uses them for cutting up chicken's guts and splitting gizzards – they disgust me.

'Mélie, tomorrow you're to buy me a pair of cutting-out scissors.'

It was a long and difficult job. A hairdresser would have done it quicker and better but my misanthropy concerning everything to do with Paris was still too acute not to shudder at the thought. Oh my poor locks, all cut off at ear-level! The ones in front, amusingly curled, didn't look too bad but I felt thoroughly miserable and furious when I saw, in two glasses, that thin white nape under the stiff little ends that were only slowly making up their minds to grow into spirals, like balsam pods that, when they've shot out their seeds, curl up little by little into corkscrews and dry that shape.

Before I had consented to put one foot out-of-doors, the human species irrupted into my home, represented by the concierge. Exasperated by hearing the Breton servant unjustly beating her unfortunate little dog every morning, I'd spied on her and poured half my big water-jug over her coif.

Five minutes later, enter the portress, a dirty, long-winded woman who had once been handsome. Papa being absent, she stared with some surprise at this pale, arrogant little girl. 'Mademoiselle, the Breton girl has said someone emptied a pail . . .' – 'I did. What of it?' – 'She says as how it's a reason for her to put up a complaint . . .' – 'My nerves can't put up with *her*. Besides, if she starts beating the dog again, she'll get something worse than water. Do I tell her employers that she spits in the breakfast-cups and blows her nose on the table napkins? If she'd prefer that, she'd better say so!' And the Breton girl has, at last, left that poor dog in peace. Moreover, you know, I've never seen her spit in the cups or blow her nose on the napkins. But she looks perfectly capable of doing so. Besides, as we say at home, she *repulses* me. Isn't that what's called a 'generous lie'?

My first outing took place in March. A sharp sun and an acid wind; Papa and myself in a cab with pneumatic tyres. In the red cloak I wore at Montigny and my astrakhan cap I looked like a poor little boy in skirts. (And all my shoes have grown so big!) We took a slow walk in the Luxembourg, where my noble father entertained me with the comparative merits of the Nationale and the Sainte-Geneviève Libraries. The wind dazed me, so did the sun. I thought the big, smooth, tree-lined walks really beautiful but the quantities of children and the absence of weeds shocked me, the one quite as much as the other.

'In re-reading the proofs of my great *Treatise*', Papa told me, 'I realized there was still a great deal more delving to be done. I'm astonished, myself, at the superficiality of certain parts. Don't you think it extraordinary, that, with my mental precision, I've only been able to touch on certain important points – of fascinating interest, I venture to say – relating to minute species? But this is no subject for a little girl.'

Little girl! Won't he ever condescend to notice that I'm forging ahead fast, leaving my seventeen years behind me? As to minute species, goodness me, I couldn't care less for them! Major species, ditto!

What lots of children, what lots of children! Shall I have as many children as that one day? And who is the gentleman who will inspire me to perpetrate them with him? Ugh, ugh! It's odd how chaste my imagination and my feelings are since my illness. What would people think of a Great *Treatise* – (my work!) – *on the elevating influence of cerebral fevers on young girls?* My poor little Luce . . . How far advanced the trees are here! The lilacs are shooting out tender leaves. Back there, back there . . . you can still only see brown and varnished

16

buds, at the most some wood-anemones, if that!

On returning from my walk I noticed that the Rue Jacob obstinately maintained its sordid aspect with its pavements freely used as spittoons. Indifferent to the flattery of my faithful Mélie, who pretended that the walk had put back some roses into her 'girlie's cheeks (she's a brazen liar, my faithful Mélie), and depressed by this Paris spring that made me dream too much of the other, the real one, I lay down on my bed, tired out. Then I got up and wrote a letter to Luce. When I'd sealed my letter, I realized, too late, that the poor little goose wouldn't understand a word of it. For it means nothing whatever to her that What's-his-name, the new tenant of our hose at Montigny, has lopped the branches of the big walnut-tree because they were trailing on the ground and that the Fredonnes wood is already hazy (you can see it from the School) with the green mist of young shoots! Luce won't be able to tell me, either, whether the corn is springing well or whether the violets at the west fork of the lane that leads to Vrimes are forward or late with their leaves. All she will notice is the unsentimental tone of my letter. She won't understand why I give her so few details about my life in Paris and why the news of my health is confined to this: 'I've been ill for two months, but am getting better.' It's to Claire, my co-First Communicant, that I ought to have written! Today, she would be looking after her sheep in the field at Vrimes or near the Matignons wood, a big cloak over her shoulders and her little round head, with its soft eyes, protected by a scarf coquettishly pinned up like a mantilla. Her sheep would be straying, restrained with difficulty by the good dog Lisette, and Claire would be absorbed in a yellow-back novel, one of the ones I had left her when I went away.

So I wrote Claire a nice, affectionate, commonplace letter. French composition: *Letter from a young girl to her friend to tell of her arrival in Paris.* Oh Mademoiselle! Red-haired and vindictive Mademoiselle, I'm still a little feverish and I can hear your cutting voice, so effective in suppressing all disorder. What are you doing with your little Aimée at this very moment? I can imagine, I can imagine quite well: and imagining it sends up my 'temperature'. . .

17

THREE

PAPA, WHOSE THOUGHTS I had turned in the direction of
Aunt Coeur, began, during the next few days, to express faint
suggestions of taking me to see her. I emitted loud screams to
frighten him.

'Go and see my Aunt? Well, of all the ideas! With my hair
like this and my face like this and not one single new frock!
Papa, it's enough to jeopardize my future and wreck my
prospects of marriage!'

(I needn't have protested so much. The eighteenth-century
features resumed their serenity.)

'Three dozen herds of swine! I like it devilish well, your
cropped hair! No, what I really mean . . . Well, the fact is I'm
revising a difficult chapter at the moment. I need at least
another week on it.'

(Things were going well.)

'Hi, Mélie, you great lazy slut, stir your stumps and look
sharp about it! I've got to get hold of a dressmaker.'

One was discovered, who came to 'take my orders'. She is
an old woman who lives in the house and her name is
Poullanx. She has scruples, she's easily alarmed, she doesn't
like tight skirts, and she ostentatiously parades an old-
fashioned honesty. When she had finished a perfectly simply
blue cloth dress with fine little tucks on the bodice and a
collar, edged with stitching, that came right up to my ears (I
can show my neck later on when I've grown plumper), she
brought me back all the bits and pieces of stuff, even little
snippets three centimetres wide. She's a dreadful woman with

her Jansenist way of disapproving of the 'immodest dresses'
that are all the rage at the moment!

There's nothing like a new dress for making me want to go
out. But, however much I brush my hair, it doesn't grow fast.
Little by little, the activity of the old Claudine is beginning to
reappear. Besides, the fact that there are plenty of bananas
about helps to make life bearable. By buying them ripe and
letting them rot just a little, bananas are sheer heaven, like
eating Liberty velvet! Fanchette thinks they smell disgusting.

During this last fortnight, I received an answer from Luce; a
letter in pencil which, I admit, staggered me.

> *My darling Claudine,*
>
> *You've taken ages to think of me! You really might have
> thought of me sooner, to give me a little strength to bear all
> the tortures I've been through. I failed in my Entrance
> Exam to the Teachers' Training College and, from that day
> to this, my sister has made me pay for it. For the least thing,
> she hits me on the head hard enough to dislocate my neck
> and she refuses to let me have any shoes. I can't ask my
> mother to let me go back home, she'd beat me too much.
> And it's no good looking to Mademoiselle to protect me
> (she's still as crazy as ever about my sister who's led her a
> pretty dance). I'm writing to you a few lines at a time. I
> don't want her to pinch my letter. When you were here,
> those two were a little afraid of you. Now everything's gone
> – everything went with you, and I'd say good-bye to this
> world if I weren't so frightened of killing myself. I don't
> know what I'm going to do but things can't go on like this.
> I shall run away, I'll go goodness knows where. Don't
> laugh at me, Claudine. Oh, if I'd only got you here, even if
> only to beat me, life would still be worth living. The two
> Jauberts and Anaïs are at the Training College. Marie
> Belhomme is serving in a shop. There are four new girls
> who are squits and, as to the violets, I don't know whether
> they're ahead of time – it's so long since I went for a walk.
> Good-bye, Claudine darling, if you can find some way of
> making me less miserable or of coming to see me, please do,*

*it would be an act of charity. I kiss your lovely hair and
your two eyes that didn't love me a bit, and your whole
face, and your white neck. Don't laugh at me, it isn't any
silly little misery to be joked about that's making me cry.*

Your
Luce.

What are they doing to her, those two horrid women? My
poor, inconsistent little Luce, too bad to be good and too
cowardly to be bad, I couldn't, all the same, have brought you
with me! (besides, I didn't want to). But you've no more
peppermints, no more chocolate, and no more Claudine. The
new School, the opening of it by the Minister, Doctor
Dutertre . . . How far away I am from all that! Doctor
Dutertre, you are the only man up to now who's dared to kiss
me – and on the corner of the mouth, too. You excited me and
you frightened me: is that all I'm to hope for, to a greater
degree, from the man who will definitely carry me away? As
regards practical notions of love, it's a trifle meagre. Luckily
my theory is far more complete, though there are some
obscure patches in it. For even Papa's library can't teach me
everything.

Well, that is more or less the summary of my first months
in Paris. My 'fair-copy book', as we used to say at school, is
up to date; it shouldn't be difficult for me to keep it so. I
haven't got much to do here. I'm making some charming little
chemises for my always needy wardrobe and some little
knickers (closed ones). I brush my hair – it's so soon done
nowadays – I comb my white Fanchette, who has hardly any
fleas left since she became a Parisienne, and install her with
her flat cushion on the window-sill so that she can take the air.
Yesterday she caught sight of the fat – how can I put it? –
impaired tom belonging to the concierge and muttered
nameless insults at him, from the height of her third storey, in
the slightly hoarse, peasant voice of an ex-outdoor cat. Mélie
looks after her health and, to prevent constipation, brings her
pots of catmint which the poor darling devours. Does she
dream of the garden, and of the great chestnut-tree we so
often climbed together? I think she does. But she loves me so

much she would live with me in the filthiest of hovels.

Escorted by Mélie, I've sampled the charms of the big shops. People stare at me in the street because I'm pale and thin, with short, bushy hair, and because Mélie wears a Fresnois peasant coif. Am I at last going to experience the covetous glances of those famous 'old gentleman' who follow young girls? We'll see about that later on: at the moment, I'm busy.

I've principally been engaged in studying the different smells in the Louvre and Bon Marché. In the linen department, it's intoxicating. Oh Anaïs! You, who used to eat samples of sheets and handkerchiefs, this is your spiritual home! That sugary smell of new blue cottons, does it thrill me or make me want to vomit? Both, I think. Shame on flannel and woollen blankets! They smell exactly like rotten eggs. The smell of new shoes is by no means to be despised, neither is that of leather purses. But they can't compete with the heavenly odour of the thick blue tracing-paper used for embroidery which consoles one for the sickening, cloying smell of the soaps and the scents . . .

Claire has answered my letter, too. Once again, she's extremely happy. This time, she really *has* found true love. And she informs me she's going to get married. At seventeen, she's really and truly 'settling down'! A mean little feeling of annoyance made me shrug my shoulders. (Now, now Claudine, my dear, how vulgar of you!) *He's so handsome,* Claire wrote, *that I'm never tired of looking at him. His eyes are stars and his beard is so soft! And he's so strong – honestly, I don't weigh more than a feather in his arms! I still don't know when we're going to get married. Mamma thinks I'm ever so much too young. But I'm imploring her to let me as soon as possible. How blissfully happy I shall be to be his wife!* She enclosed a little photograph of the Loved One with these ravings; he's a broad fellow who looks thirty-five, with an honest, placid face, kind little eyes, and a bushy beard.

In her ecstasy, she completely forgot to tell me whether the violets at the west fork of the lane that leads to Vrimes . . .

FOUR

NO GETTING OUT of it, we've got to go and call on Aunt Coeur, otherwise she'll be annoyed with us when she knows we've been in Paris so long, and I hate family rows. Papa suggested the ingenious idea of warning her in advance of our visit but I fiercely dissuaded him.

'You know, we oughtn't to spoil the pleasure of the surprise. Considering we've been her three months without letting her know, let's go the whole hog and spring it on her in a dramatic way!'

(In that case, if she were out, at least we'd have gained a little time. And we should have done our duty.)

We set off, Papa and I, about four o'clock. Papa was, quite frankly, sublime with his overcoat with the ample red ribbon in the buttonhole and that top-hat whose brim is far too wide and that dominant nose and that tri-coloured beard. His whole appearance – suggesting a retired army officer awaiting the return of the rightful King of France – and his childish, ecstatic expression excited the enthusiasm of the urchins of the neighbourhood and they greeted him with cheers.

I was indifferent to this popularity. I had put on my new dress of perfectly plain blue cloth and on my hair – what was left of it – I'd carefully poised my round black felt hat with the feathers, artfully arranging some curls on my temples and pulling some forward over my eyebrows. My apprehension over the visit made me look ill; it still doesn't take much to make me do that!

Aunt Coeur lives in a magnificent, unattractive new block of flats in the Avenue de Wagram. The rapid lift made Papa uneasy. And, personally, I rather disliked all those white walls and stairs and woodwork. And Madame Coeur was 'in'. What bad luck!

The drawing-room where we waited a minute or two desperately carried on the whiteness of the staircase. White painted woodwork, frail white furniture, white cushions with light-coloured flowers, white chimney-piece. Great heavens, there wasn't one single dark corner! And *I* can't feel safe and comfortable except in dim rooms and dark woods and deep, heavy armchairs! That 'eighteenth-century' white of the windows sets one's teeth on edge like the noise of zinc being scraped . . .

Enter Aunt Coeur. She was astounded, but extremely agreeable. And how she prided herself on her august resemblance! She had the Empress Eugénie's distinguished nose, her smooth, heavy swathes of greying hair, her slightly drooping smile. Not for anything in the world would she have given up her low (and artificial) chignon or her very full gathered skirt, or the little lace scarf that *flirted* (ha! ha!) round her shoulders that were drooping, like her smile. My good Aunt, how Your Majesty, who reigned before 1870, clashes with this drawing-room all done up in whipped cream that couldn't be more pure 1900!

But she was charming, Aunt Coeur! She spoke a polished French that intimidated me, exclaimed over our unexpected move – it certainly *was* unexpected! – and never stopped staring at me. I couldn't get over hearing someone call Papa by his Christian name. And she used the formal *vous* to her brother.

'But, Claude, this child . . . incidentally she's charming and a completely individual type . . . hasn't really recovered yet. You must have nursed her in your own rough and ready way, poor little thing! What I simply can't understand is why it never entered you head to send for me! You're just the same as ever!'

23

Papa took his sister's remonstrances very ill, and he so seldom jibs at anything. They obviously seldom see eye to eye with each other and start bickering at once. I began to get interested.

'Wilhelmine, I looked after my daughter perfectly adequately. Incidentally, I had a great deal on my mind, and I can't think of everything.'

'And this idea of living in the Rue Jacob! My dear, the new neighbourhoods are far healthier, far airier and far better built, and they're no more expensive. I simply don't understand you . . . Look here, at 145B . . . just a few yards from here, there's a delightful flat, and we'd be practically on each other's doorsteps . . . We could be always running in and out . . . it would be nice for Claudine and for you too.'

(Papa leapt in his chair.)

'Live here? My dear girl, you're the most exquisite woman on earth, but I'd rather be shot than live in your company!'

(Oh, well done, Papa! This time I laughed wholeheartedly and Aunt Coeur seemed stupefied by my being so little upset by their disagreements.)

'Little girl, wouldn't you rather have a pretty, light flat like this than be on that dirty Left Bank where no nice people live?'

'Aunt, I think I prefer the Rue Jacob and the flat there, because light rooms depress me.'

She raised her arched, deliberately Spanish-looking eyebrows under her concentric wrinkles and seemed to attribute my demented words to my state of health. Then she began to talk to Papa about their family.

'I have my grandson, Marcel, living here with me – you know, poor Ida's son (??). He's doing his philosophy course and he's about Claudine's age. I shan't say a word about *him*,' she added, radiant. 'He's a treasure for a grandmother. You'll see him in a moment: he comes home at five and I'm longing to show him to you.'

Papa said 'Yes' and looked impressed. But I could see that he hadn't the faintest notion who Ida was or who Marcel was, and that he was already bored at having rediscovered his family! I was thoroughly enjoying myself! But my amusement

24

was entirely inward and I didn't shine in conversation. Papa was dying to go and could only resist the temptation by talking about his great treatise on Malacology. At last, a door banged, there was a light step and the heralded Marcel entered . . . Heavens, how pretty he was!

I gave him my hand without saying a word, I was staring at him so much. I'd never seen anything so charming! But he was a *girl*! A slip of a girl in breeches! Fair hair, rather long, parted on the right, a complexion like Luce's, blue eyes like a little English girl's and no more moustache than I had. He was blushing, he spoke softly, keeping his head a little on one side and looking down at the ground. You could have eaten him! Papa, however, seemed insensible to so much far from manly charm, wheras Aunt Coeur devoured her grandson with her eyes.

'You're back very late, darling. I hope nothing happened to you?'

'No, Grandmother,' replied the little wonder sweetly, raising his pure eyes.

Papa, who continued to be a hundred miles away, vaguely questioned Marcel about his studies. And I went on staring at this pretty sugar-stick of a cousin! *He*, on the contrary, didn't so much as look at me, and, if my admiration hadn't been so disinterested, I should have felt slightly humiliated. Aunt Coeur, who had exultantly observed the effect produced by her cherub, tried to bring us together a little:

'Marcel, Claudine is the same age as you are, you know. You'll be nice companions for each other. The Easter holidays will soon be here.'

I made a brisk movement forward to show that I was all in favour; the boy, surprised at my eagerness, looked up at me with his blue eyes and replied with tempered enthusiasm:

'I'd like that very much, Grandmother, if Madam – if Claudine is willing.'

After that, there was no stopping Aunt Coeur. She told us at length about the virtues of her precious darling. 'I never even had to raise my voice.' She made us stand shoulder to shoulder, Marcel was all that much taller! (*All that much* was three centimetres, hardly worth making such a terrific fuss about!) The treasure condescended to laugh and to become a little livelier. He straightened his tie in front of the glass. He was dressed like a pretty fashion-plate. And that walk, that swaying, gliding walk! That way of turning round, pivoting on one hip! No, he was really too good-looking! I was startled out of my contemplation by the following question from Aunt Coeur. 'Claude, you'll both dine here, won't you?'

'Good Lord, no!' exploded Pap, who was dying of boredom. 'I've got an appointment at home with . . . with what's-his-name who's bringing me some documents, some documents for my treatise. Come along, child, we must be off!'

'I'm *so* sorry, and tomorrow I'm not dining at home. I'm rather booked-up this season, I've stupidly gone and accepted invitations from all and sundry. How about Thursday? Just ourselves, of course. Claude, are you listening to me?'

'I'm hanging on your lips, my dear, but I'm damnably late. Till Thursday, Wilhelmine. Good-bye, young Paul . . . no, Jacques.'

I said good-bye too, unwillingly. Marcel saw us to the door, very polite and correct, and kissed my glove.

We returned in silence through the lighted streets. I haven't got used yet to being out-of-doors at that hour, and the lights and the dark passers-by made me nervous and brought a lump into my throat. I was in a hurry to get home. Papa, released from the miseries of his visit, gaily hummed songs of the First Empire. '*Nine months later, a sweet pledge of love.*'

The soft lamplight and the table laid for dinner revived my spirits and loosened my tongue.

'Mélie, I've seen my aunt. Mélie, I've seen my cousin. He's so-so . . . his hair's combed smooth as smooth . . . he's got a short parting . . . his name's Marcel.'

'Now then, my pet, now then! You're defeating me. Come along, eat up your nice soupy. So you'll have a young man, and high time too!'

'You big fathead! Silly idiot, do you have to be so dense? He's *not* a young man! Why, I don't even know him! Oh, you make me sick. I'm going to my room.'

And, believe it or not, I *did* go to my room! The very idea that a little mother's darling like Marcel could be a lover for *me*! If I found him so attractive and made so little secret of it, it was precisely because he seemed to me no more of a man than Luce herself.

The effect of once more seeing people who live like everyone else and talking to someone other than Franchette and Mélie was to make me slightly, but rather pleasantly, feverish and keep me awake part of the night. The sort of fancies one has at midnight danced through my head. I was frightened of not knowing what to say to the amiable Aunt Coeur who had stepped straight out of a Winterhalter painting; she'd taken me for a dolt. Goodness, sixteen years at Montigny, of which ten were spent at school, hardly develop the gift of repartee! You emerged from that with just enough vocabulary to call Anaïs names and to pet Luce. That pretty little girl of a Marcel probably couldn't every say 'Shut up'. He'd make fun of me on Thursday if I skinned my bananas with my teeth. And what should I wear for that dinner? I hadn't got an evening frock, I'd have to wear the one I wore for the opening of the Schools: white muslin with a cross-over fichu. He'd think it very dull and ordinary.

The result was that having gone to sleep last night in openmouth admiration of that boy whose trousers haven't a single wrinkle in them, I woke up this morning with a strong desire to slap his face. All the same, if Anaïs set eyes on him, she's be quite capable of raping him! The gawky Anaïs, with her yellow face and her brusque gestures, raping little Marcel made a funny picture. It made me laugh in spite of myself as I went into Papa's book-lair.

To my surprise, Papa wasn't alone. He was talking to a gentleman, a young gentleman who looked quite intelligent and had a square beard. It appeared he was a 'first-class man', Monsieur Maria, you know, who discovered the underground caves at X . . . Papa had met him in some boring place, the Geographical Society or somewhere else in the Sorbonne and had got excited about these caves – they might contain some hypothetical fossilized slugs! He indicated me to him by saying: 'This is Claudine', as he might have said: 'This is Leo XIII, of course you know he's the Pope.' At which, Monsieur Maria bowed as if he perfectly understood the situation. A man like that who fiddles about all the time in caves – I'm perfectly sure he must smell of snails.

After lunch, I asserted my independence.

'Papa, I'm going out.'

(This did not go down as well as I should have expected.)

'Going out? With Mélie, I presume?'

'No, she's got some mending to do.

'What! You want to go out all by yourself?'

I opened my eyes as wide as saucers.

'Gracious, of course I'm going out by myself – what's wrong?'

'What's wrong is that, in Paris, young girls . . .'

'Look here, Papa, you must try and be consistent. At Montigny, I used to wander about the woods all the time. I should have thought that was lots more dangerous than walking along a Paris pavement.'

'There's something in that. But I might foresee dangers of another kind in Paris. Read the papers.'

'Fie, fie, father, it is an offence to your daughter even to entertain such a supposition!' (Papa did not look as if he understood this elegant allusion. No doubt he neglects Molière as not being sufficiently concerned with slugs.) 'Besides, I never read the sensational news items. I'm going to the Louvre – the shop, not the picture gallery. I must be tidy for Aunt Coeur's dinner-party. I haven't got any fine stockings, and my white shoes are shabby. Gimme some lovely money . . . I've only a hundred and six sous.'

(In Fresnois they reckon in sous up to six francs, with the exception of sixty sous which they call three francs like anywhere else.)

FIVE

WELL, AFTER ALL, it's not terrible going out alone in Paris.
I brought back some very interesting observations from my
little walk: (I) it's much warmer in Montigny; (2) your nose is
all black inside when you get home; (3) people stare at you if
you stand still in front of a newspaper kiosk; (4) people also
stare at you when you don't let yourself be disrespectfully
treated on the pavement.

Let me narrate the incident that gave rise to observation (4).
A very good-looking gentleman followed me in the Rue des
Saints-Pères. During the first quarter of an hour, inner
jubilation of Claudine. Followed by a very good-looking
gentleman, just like in Albert Guillaume's pictures! Second
quarter of an hour . . . the gentleman's step came closer; I
hastened mine, but he kept his distance. Third quarter of an
hour; the gentleman passed me, pinching my behind with a
detached expression. A leap in the air from Claudine who
raised her umbrella and brought it down on the gentleman's
head with a typical Fresnois vigour. Gentleman's hat in the
gutter, immense delight of passers-by, disappearance of
Claudine, overwhelmed by her too sensational success. Aunt
Coeur is very nice. She's sent me, with a friendly note, a
necklace, a thin gold chain with little round pearls strung on
it at intervals of ten centimetres. Fanchette thinks this piece of
jewellery is charming; she has already flattened two of the
links and she bites the pearls with her big teeth, like an expert
in precious stones.

*

While I was getting ready for the Thursday dinner-party, I thought about my décolletage. It was very, very modest, but suppose I was going to look too thin? Sitting in my tub, quite naked, I noticed that I had put on a little flesh, but I still needed to put on more. What luck that my neck had stayed round and firm! That saved me. It was a pity about the two little salt-cellars at the base, but they couldn't be helped. I wasted time in the hot water, counting the little bones in my back, measuring whether I was the same length from my groin to my feet as from my groin to my forehead, pinching my right calf because I could feel it in my left shoulder blade. (At every pinch, a funny little sting behind one's shoulder.) And what sheer bliss to be able to hook my feet behind my neck! As that dirty great gangling Anaïs used to say: 'It must be frightfully amusing to be able to bite one's toenails!'

Good heaven, how tiny my breasts were! (At school, we called them bubs and Mélie, says titties.) I thought of our 'Competitions' of three years ago, during our rare Thursday walks.

In a clearing of the wood, in a sunken path, we used to sit in a circle – we four big ones – and we used to open our bodices. Anaïs (what cheek!) used to display a morsel of lemon-coloured skin, swell out her stomach and say impudently: *'They've* come on like anything since last month!' Nothing of the sort! The Sahara desert! Luce, pink and white in her coarse schoolgirl chemise – long-sleeved chemises without so much as a scallop, that's the rule – uncovered a hardly discernible 'centre valley' and two small pink points like Fanchette's nipples. And Claudine? A little arched chest but about as much breasts as a slightly plump boy. Well, after all, at fourteen! The exhibition over, we fastened up our bodices again, each of us with the inner conviction that we had much more of *them* than the three others.

My white muslin dress, well-ironed by Mélie, still seemed attractive enough to me not to feel peevish when I put it on. My poor beautiful hair no longer cascaded over it right down to my hips, but it stood out so amusingly round my head that I didn't languish too much over my vanished mane, that night. Ten thousand herds of swine! – to use Papa's pet expression –

at all costs, I mustn't forget my gold chain!

'Mélie, is Papa getting dressed?'

'He's getting dressed all right. Overdoing it, if you ask me. He's bust three stiff collars already. Run along and tie his tie.'

I hurried to do so. My noble father had got himself up in a slightly, in fact a *very*, old-fashioned evening suit, but it was impossible for him not to look imposing.

'Hurry up, hurry up, Papa, it's half past seven. Mélie, you give Fanchette her dinner. My red cloak, and let's be off!'

The white drawing-room, with electric bulbs in all the corners, made me feel that, any moment, I might have an epileptic fit. Papa thinks as I do; he loathes this iced-cake décor so dear to his sister Wilhelmine and said so in no uncertain manner.

'Believe it or not, I'd have myself flogged in public rather than sleep inside this cream bun.'

But the pretty Marcel appeared and beautified everything with his presence. How charming he looked! Light and slim in a dinner-jacket, his hair moonlight fair, his translucent skin velvety under the lights like the inside of a convolvulus. While he was saying good evening to us, I noticed that his pale blue eyes were giving me a swift inspection.

Aunt Coeur followed him, dazzling. That dress of pearl-grey silk with flounces of black Chantilly lace, was its date 1867 or 1900? 1867, more likely, only a household-cavalryman must have sat on the crinoline and flattened it somewhat. The two grey bandeaux were very thick and very smooth; in the old days, she must have studied that pale blue gaze under the drooping, worn eyelids so thoroughly from the Comtesse de Téba that it had become second nature. She had a gliding walk, she wore sleeves set into deep armholes, and she showed herself full of . . . urbanity. 'Urbanity' is a noun that suits her as well as her bandeaux.

No other guests beside ourselves. But, goodness me, how they dress up at Aunt Coeur's! At Montigny, I used to dine in my school pinafore and Papa used to keep on the indescribable garment – cloak, overcoat, coachman's cape, a mongrel product of all three – that he'd put on first thing in the morning to feed his slugs in. If one wears low necks for an intimate family meal, what on earth shall I put on for big dinner-parties? Perhaps my chemise with the pink ribbon shoulder straps . . .

(Claudine, old thing, enough of these disgressions! You must try and eat correctly and not say, when you're handed a dish you don't like: 'Take it away, I think it's disgusting!')

Naturally, I was seated beside Marcel. Oh horror, oh misery! The dining-room was white too! White and yellow, but the effect was just as bad. And the crystal and the flowers and the electric light . . . it all made such a shindy on the table, you could positively *hear* it. Honestly, all those sparkles of light gave me an impression of noise.

Marcel, under Aunt Coeur's adoring eye, behaved like a society debutante and asked if I was enjoying myself in Paris. At first, a savage 'no' was all he got in reply. But soon I became a little more human, because I was eating a little patty with truffles that would have consoled a widow the day after her bereavement, so I condescended to explain myself.

'You see, I'm quite sure I shall enjoy myself later on. But, up to now, I find it terribly hard to get used to not seeing any leaves. Third floors in Paris don't exactly abound in green "tillers".'

'In green . . . *what*?'

'In "tillers". It's what we call them in Fresnois,' I added with a certain pride.

'Oh, it's a Fresnois word, is it? Rather unusual! Gr-r-een tillers,' he repeated teasingly, rolling the *r*.

'I forbid you to mimic me! If you imagine it's more elegant, your Parisian *r* that you rumble in the depths of your throat as if you were gargling!'

'Ugh, you dirty little thing! Are your girl friends like you?'

'I didn't have any girl friends. I don't much care for having girl friends. Luce had a soft skin, but that isn't enough.'

'Luce had a soft skin . . . What a funny way of judging people!'

'Why funny? From the moral point of view, Luce simply doesn't exist. I'm considering her from the physical point of view and I tell you she has green eyes and a soft skin.'

'Did you love each other very much?'

(That pretty, vicious face! What wouldn't one say to him to see those eyes light up! Shame on you, you naughty little boy!)

'No, I didn't love her in the least. *She* did, yes. She cried like anything when I went away.'

'But, then, which one did you like better?'

My calmness emboldened Marcel. Perhaps he took me for a goose and would gladly have asked me more definite questions but the grown-ups stopped talking for a moment while a manservant with a clerical face changed the plates and we stopped, too. There was already a touch of complicity between us.

Aunt Coeur's tired blue gaze wandered from Marcel to myself.

'Claude,' she said to Papa, 'look how those two children set each other off. Your daughter's ivory skin and her hair with those bronze lights in it and her deep eyes – all that brunette look some little girls have who aren't really brunettes – make my cherub look fairer than ever. Don't you agree?'

'Yes,' replied Papa with conviction. 'He's much more of a girl than she is.'

Her cherub and I lowered our eyes as becomes children bursting at once with pride and a desperate desire to giggle. And the dinner pursued its course without further confidences. Moreover, a delicious tangerine ice detached me from all other preoccupations.

I returned to the drawing-room on Marcel's arm. And all at once, no one seemed to know what to do. Aunt Coeur appeared to have some serious things to say to Papa and got rid of us.

'Marcel, my darling, go and show Claudine over the flat. Be nice – try and make her feel a little at home.'

'Come along,' said the 'darling', 'I'll take you to see my room.'

It was white, too, just as I had expected. White and green, with slender reeds on a white ground. But so much whiteness eventually aroused in me a secret desire to upset inkpots – heaps of inkpots – over it, to scribble in charcoal all over the walls, to dirty that distemper with blood from a cut

33

finger . . . Heavens, how perverse I'd become in an all-white flat!

I went straight to the chimneypiece on which I saw a photograph-frame. Excitedly, Marcel switched on an electric light just over our heads.

'That's my best friend . . . Charlie . . . Almost like a brother. Isn't he good-looking?'

Much too good-looking, in fact. Dark eyes, with curving lashes, the merest hint of a black moustache above a tender mouth, hair parted at the side, like Marcel's.

'I certainly agree he's handsome! Nearly as good-looking as you are,' I said sincerely.

'Oh, *much* better!' he exclaimed fervently. 'The photograph can't do justice to his white skin and his black hair. And he's such a charming *person* . . .'

And so on and so on. That pretty Dresden china figure was coming to life at last. I listened, without flinching, to the panegyric of the magnificent Charlie, and when Marcel, slightly embarrassed, regained his self-possession, I looked completely convinced and answered quite naturally: 'I understand perfectly. You're his Luce.'

He took a step backwards and, under the light. I saw his pretty features harden and his sensitive skin turn imperceptibly paler.

'His Luce? Claudine, what do you mean by that?'

With the boldness derived from two glasses of champagne, I shrugged my shoulders and said:

'But of course. His Luce, his pet, his darling, whatever you call it! One's only got to look at you – do you *look* like a man? That's just why I found you so pretty!'

And as he stood there, perfectly still, staring at me almost icily, I went up closer to him and added, smiling right into his face:

'Marcel, I find you just as pretty at this very moment, believe me. Now, do I look like someone who wants to upset you? I tease you, but I'm not spiteful and there are lots of things I know perfectly well how to keep quiet about and to listen to without telling anyone else. I shall never be the female cousin whose unfortunate male cousin feels he's forced to

34

make love to her as they do in books. May I remind you,' I went on, laughing, 'that you're the grandson of my aunt, what's called my "Breton nephew"? Marcel, it would be practically incest!'

My 'nephew' decided to laugh, but he didn't really want to.

'My dear Claudine, I quite agree that you're not like the little female cousins in "nice" novels. But I'm afraid that, at Montigny, you've got into the habit of making rather, well – risky – jokes. Suppose there'd been someone listening to us. Grandmother, for example – or your father . . .'

'I was only giving you tit for tat,' I said very sweetly, 'And I didn't think it necessary to attract the family's attention when you kept plying me with questions about Luce.'

'You had more to lose than I had, if you *had* attracted their attention!'

'Do you think so? I very much doubt it. In the case of girls, those little diversions are just called "school-girls' nonsense". But when I comes to boys of seventeen, it's almost a disease . . .'

He made a violent gesture with his hand.

'You read too much! Young girls have too much imagination to really understand what they read, even if they do come from Montigny.'

I'd managed things badly. That wasn't in the least what I was driving at.

'Have I made you angry, Marcel? I'm a clumsy idiot! All I wanted to do was to prove to you that I wasn't a goose, that I could understand – how can I put it? – *appreciate* certain things. Look, Marcel, you can't really expect me to see you as a great raw-boned schoolboy with enormous feet who'll turn into the perfect type of N.C.O. one day. Just look at yourself! Aren't you, thank heaven, almost exactly like the very prettiest of my schoolfriends? Give me your hand . . .'

He really ought to have been a girl! All he did was to smile furtively at my over-enthusiastic compliments. He held out his little manicured paw with quite good grace.

'Claudine, you wicked Claudine, let's get back to them quickly. We'll go through Grandmother's bedroom. I'm not angry any more, only a little flabbergasted still. Let me think things over . . . It seems to me you aren't too bad a *boy* . . .'

His sarcasm didn't upset me a bit! To see him sulking and then smiling again, was pure pleasure. I didn't pity his friend with the sweeping eyelashes in the least and I wished them plenty of quarrels with my blessing.

Looking extremely natural – almost unnaturally natural – we continued the tour of the estate. What joy, Aunt Coeur's room was adequate (ghastly word!) to its owner! In it, she had assembled – or exiled – all the furniture that must have been in her room when she was a girl, all the souvenirs of her heyday. The carved rosewood bed, the red damask armchairs that all looked like Their Imperial Majesties' thrones, the tapestry prie-dieu bristling with oak carvings, the flashy imitation of a Boule desk, console tables galore – they were all there. Damask curtains dripped from the canopy of the bed and the ornate chimneypiece, a shapeless, complicated mass of cupids and acanthus leaves and gilded bronze wreaths, filled me with admiration. Marcel had a supreme contempt for this room and we disputed hotly about the modern style and the merits of beaten egg-white in interior decoration. This aesthetic wrangle allowed us to return, in a calmer frame of mind, to the drawing-room where Papa was yawning like a lion in a cage under the gentle, relentless rain of Aunt Coeur's good advice.

'Grandmother!' cried Marcel, 'Claudine's priceless! She likes your bedroom better than all the rest of the flat.'

'Funny little girl,' said my aunt, caressing me with her languid smile. 'My room's very ugly, really . . .'

'. . . But it suits you, Aunt. Don't you think your bandeaux "clash" with this drawing-room? Thank goodness, you know that perfectly well, because you've kept one little corner of your proper setting!'

It wasn't exactly a compliment, perhaps, but she got up and came over and kissed me very sweetly. Suddenly Papa leapt to his feet and consulted his watch.

'Ten thousand herds of . . . Sorry, Wilhelmine, but it's five minutes to ten and it's the first time this child has been out since her illness . . . Young man, go and order us a cab!'

Marcel went out, and quickly returned, with that quick, supple way of swinging round as he went through a doorway, bringing me my red cloak that he dropped deftly on my shoulders.

'Good-bye Aunt.'

'Good-bye, my child. I'm at home on Sundays. It would be too charming of you to come and hand round my tea at five o'clock with your friend Marcel.'

Inwardly, I curled up like a prickly hedgehog.

'I don't know how to, Aunt, I've never . . .'

'Now, now, I won't take no as an answer. I must make you into a little person who's as charming as she's pretty! Good-bye, Claude, don't shut yourself up too much in your lair – give a thought now and then to your old sister!'

At the front door, my 'nephew' kissed my wrist a little more lingeringly and accompanied his 'Till Sunday' with a knowing smile and a delicious pout and . . . that was that.

All the same, I'd been on the very verge of quarrelling with that boy! Claudine, old thing, will you never cure yourself of that itch to meddle in things that don't concern you, that rather despicable little wish to show that you're artful and knowledgeable and understand heaps of things beyond your age? This urge to astonish people, this crave to disturb people's peace of mind and upset too-placid lives will play you a nasty trick one of these days.

I felt much more at home, back in my own room, squatting on my four-poster bed and stroking Fanchette who had begun her night without waiting for me and lay there trustingly, with her stomach upturned. But – begging your pardon, Fanchette – I recognized those smiling slumbers, those blissful hours of perpetual purring. And I also recognized that filling-out of the flanks and that exceptionally well-licked belly along which the little pink nipples stood out. Fanchette, you had fallen from virtue! But with whom? Good heaves, it was like running one's head against brick wall! A female cat who didn't go out-of-doors, the concierge's neutered tom . . . who, who could it have been? All the same, I was simply delighted. Kittens in prospect! Compared with this joyous future, even the prestige of Marcel paled.

I asked Mélie for explanations of this mysterious pregnancy. She owned up to everything.

'My lamby, this last time the poor darling did want it so cruel. Three whole days, she was in such a state, she was quite beside herself. So I asked round among the neighbours. The maid downstairs lent me a lovely husband for her, a fine striped grey. I gave him lots of milk to encourage him and our poor darling didn't have to be asked twice . . . they got together straight away.'

How she must have been pining, poor Mélie, to act as Cupid's messenger for someone, if only for the cat! She did absolutely right.

Our home has become a meeting-place for various odd people, each more astonishing and more scientific than the last. Monsieur Maria, the Cantal caves one, frequently comes along with that shy man's beard of his. When we meet in the book-lair, he bows awkwardly and makes stammering inquiries about my health, which I lugubriously assure him is 'very bad, very bad, Monsieur Maria'. I've made the acquaintance of various fat, untidy men with ribbons in their buttonholes whose lives are devoted, I understand, to the cultivation of fossils . . . Anything but exciting, Papa's friends!

SIX

AT FOUR O'CLOCK today, Marcel came to see me, 'spick and span as if he'd come straight out of a bandbox', as Mélie said. I welcomed him like the sunshine and took him into the drawing-room where he was immensely amused by the arrangement of furniture and the artificial partition created by the big curtain. 'Come along, Nephew, I'm going to show you my room.' He contemplated the narrow four-poster and the odd assortment of little bits of furniture with the slightly contemptuous gaiety that Aunt Coeur's bedroom inspired in him, but he was keenly interested in Fanchette.

'How white she is!'

'That's because I brush her every day.'

'And fat!'

'That's because she's pregnant.'

'Ah! She's . . .'

'Yes. That crazy Mélie brought her a tom-cat because Fanchette nearly went out of her mind while I was ill. The interview had fruitful results, as you see!'

My freedom in speaking about such things obviously made him uncomfortable. I began to laugh and he stared at me with a slightly shocked expression.

'Are you staring at me because I don't talk respectably? Well, that's because, down there in the country, you see cows and dogs and goats getting married very hastily and unceremoniously every day. Down there, it isn't in the least indecent.'

'What, not indecent! You know, in Zola's *La Terre*, I

realized very well it wasn't as innocent as all that. Peasants don't always watch those things in a purely detached, practical way just as part of the job of farming.'

'Your Zola just doesn't understand the first thing about the country. I don't much care for his work in general . . .'

Marcel wandered about, spying into every corner. What tiny feet he has. He discovered *The Double Mistress* on my desk and wagged his tapering finger at me.

'Claudine, Claudine, I'll tell my uncle!'

'My dear boy, he couldn't care less.'

'What an accommodating Papa. I wish Grandmother were as easy-going! Oh, that doesn't stop me reading,' he replied to the questioning thrust of my chin. 'But, for the sake of peace, I've had to pretend that I'm frightened of the dark and must have a light in my room.'

I burst out laughing.

'Frightened! You actually told her you were frightened! Weren't you ashamed?'

'Oh, what on earth does that matter! Grandmother's brought me up – and she does to this day – just like a little girl.'

Those last words reminded us so vividly of the scene two evenings ago that we both blushed (he more than I, his skin's so white!). And we were so obviously thinking of the same thing that he asked me:

'Haven't you got a photograph of Luce?'

'No; not a single one.'

'I bet that's a lie.'

'Word of honour! And anyway, you'd quite likely think she was ugly. But I'm not coy about Luce – look, here's the only letter she's written me.'

He avidly read the pathetic scrawl and this little Parisian who adored sensational news-items became impassioned.

'But it's a drama, a case of illegal restraint! Oughtn't we to get hold of someone and take legal action?'

'What a crazy idea? What on earth has it got to do with you?'

'To do with me? But, Claudine, it's a case of positive cruelty! You read it again!'

40

To read it, I leant on his fragile shoulder. He smiled, because my hair got into his ear. But I did not lean any harder. I merely said to him:

'You're not cross any more, Marcel?'

'No, no,' he said hurriedly. 'But, I implore you, do tell me all about Luce. I'll be awfully nice, if you tell me all about Luce! Look . . . I'll bring Fanchette a collar.'

'No good, she'd only eat it! My poor boy, there's nothing to tell. Besides, I'm only going to *exchange* confidences with you. Give and take, or nothing doing.'

He sulked like a girl, head down and lips pouting.

'Tell me, Marcel, do you often put that face on with your . . . your friend? Tell me his Christian name again?'

'He's called Charlie,' my 'nephew' replied, after a moment's hesitation.

'How old? Come on, come one, have I got to drag everything out of you?'

'He's eighteen, but very serious, very mature for his age. Really, the things you've been imagining!'

'Stop it. You make me fed up, d'you hear? We're not going to start all that rot again, are we? Be his girl friend as much as you like, but be a good pal to me just for once and I'll tell you all about Luce. There!'

With his disarming grace, he gently grasped my wrists.

'Oh, you *are* an angel! I've been longing for such ages to hear *real* girls' secrets. Here in Paris, girls are either women or mugs. I say Claudine, *dear* Claudine, *do* let me be your confidant!'

Was this the icy little piece of perfection of our first meeting? As he talked to me, he held out his hands and made tremendous plays with his eyes and mouth and his whole face to coax a confidence out of me; exactly as I'm sure he did when he was trying to cajole a kiss or a reconciliation. And I was suddenly tempted to invent all sorts of disgraceful things I'd done. He'd tell me others – that he almost certainly *had* done. It was rather beastly of me. But what could you expect? I couldn't get it into my head that I was playing with a boy. If he had put his arms round my waist or kissed me, I'd have scratched his eyes out by now, and that would have been the

41

end of it. The evil arose from the fact that there wasn't any danger . . .

My 'nephew' was in no mood to give me any time for reflection. He pulled me by my wrists, seated me in my tub-armchair, and settled himself on the floor on my chaff-stuffed cushion, hitching up his trousers so that they shouldn't bag at the knees.

'There, now we're nicely settled! Oh, how horrid that gloomy courtyard is! Do you mind if I draw the curtain? And now, tell me how all *that* began?'

In the long glass, I could see the two of us. I must admit we weren't ugly – I've seen worse. But what was I going to invent for him, that avid, fair-haired boy who was sitting so close to me to listen that I could see all the rays of slate-blue over periwinkle-blue that glittered in the irises of his eyes? I told myself sternly I'd only got to remember my schooldays. I needn't go as far as telling actual lies: a little exaggeration perhaps, no more.

'Oh, *I* don't know. That sort of thing doesn't have a definite beginning. It's, it's a gradual transformation of one's every-day-life, a . . .'

'. . . An *infiltration* . . .'

'Thank you, Sir. It's obvious *you* know all about it.'

'Claudine, Claudine, don't wander off into generalizations. Generalizations are so colourless. Keep your promise, tell me the whole story. First of all, you must describe Luce to me. An Introductory Chapter, only brief!'

'Luce? That's soon done. Small, brown-haired, pink and white, green slits of eyes, curling eyelashes – like yours – too small a nose and a slightly Mongol face. There, I *told* you you wouldn't like her type! Wait. Feet, hands, ankles, all very delicate. My accent, a real Fresnois accent, only more drawling. Untruthful, greedy, wheedling. She was never happy when she hadn't had her daily thrashing.'

'Her "thrashing"? Do you mean you used to beat her?'

'Certainly, that's what I mean, but you mustn't interrupt. "Silence in the Junior Class or I'll set you twice as many sums for tomorrow!" That was what Mademoiselle used to say when her dear Aimée couldn't keep her pupils in order.'

'Who was she, this Aimée?

'Mademoiselle's – the Headmistress's – Luce.'

'Right. Go on.'

'I proceed. One morning that it was our turn to break up firewood for the stove in the shed . . .'

'*What* did you say?'

'I said: one morning that it was our turn to break up firewood for the . . .'

'You actually used to break up firewood at that boarding-school?'

'It isn't a boarding-school, it's a day-school. Everyone took it in turns to break up firewood at half past seven on winter mornings, even in the coldest weather. You've no idea how splinters hurt, when it's freezing! I always had my pockets full of hot chestnuts to eat in class and to warm my hands. And the ones who had to break up the twigs used to hurry to get there early, so as to suck the icicles on the pump by the shed. And I used to bring raw chestnuts too, unsplit ones, to annoy Mademoiselle by putting them in the stove.'

'Gosh! Whoever heard of a school like that! But Luce, Luce?'

'Luce moaned more than anyone the mornings she was "on wood" and used to cling to me for consolation. "Claudine, I be froze, my hands are peeling, look see, my thumb be all scratted! Cuddle me, Claudine, my darling Claudine." And she'd snuggle up under my cloak and kiss me.'

'How? How?' Marcel impatiently inquired. He was listening with his mouth half-open and his cheeks flushed. 'How did she cud . . . kiss you?'

'On the cheeks, of course, and on the neck,' I said, as if I'd suddenly become mentally deficient.

'Get away with you, you're just a woman like all the rest!'

'That's most definitely not what Luce thought.' (I put my hands on his shoulders to make him keep still.) 'Don't get cross, the horrors will come all in good time!'

'Claudine, one minute. Didn't it upset you, her talking dialect?'

'Dialect? You'd have found dialect positively attractive, my young Parisian, spoken in that tearful, sing-song voice and coming from that mouth under the red hood that hid her forehead and ears. All you could see was a little pink nose and two cheeks like velvety peaches – even the cold didn't take the colour out of them! To blazes with dialect!'

'What passion, Claudine! Anyone can see you haven't forgotten her yet.'

'Then, one morning, Luce put a letter in my hand.'

'Ah! At last! Where is it, that letter?'

'I tore it up and gave it back to Luce.'

'That's not true!'

'So you call me a liar, do you? All right, I shall pack you off to Avenue Wagram to see if your cake's nicely browned.'

'Sorry! I only meant I could hardly believe it.'

'All right, you little beast! Yes, I did give it back to her. Because it suggested things that weren't . . . well, proper. There!'

'Claudine, in heaven's name, don't keep me on tenterhooks.'

'She wrote: *My darling, if you'd only be my best friend, I don't think I'd have anything in the world left to wish for. We should be as happy as my sister Aimée is with Mademoiselle, and I'd be grateful to you my whole life. I love you so much, I think you're so pretty. Your skin is softer than that yellow powder on lily petals. I even love it when you scratch me because you've got little cold nails . . . All that sort of thing, you know.'*

'Ah? . . . That artless humility . . . But, you know, it's adorable!'

My 'nephew' was in a state of tremendous excitement. If that's what's meant by an impressionable nature, he certainly has one, all right! He wasn't looking at me any more; his eyelashes were fluttering, his cheeks stained with crimson, and his pretty nose had turned pale. I'd never seen anyone in the grip of that particular emotion except Luce, but how much more beautiful *he* was! I suddenly thought: 'If he looked up, if he put his arms around me at this precise minute, what should I do?' A little caterpillar crept up my spine. He raised his lashes, thrust his head nearer and passionately implored:

'What next, Claudine, what next?'

He wasn't excited by *me*, of course, but by my story and the details he hoped to hear! Claudine, my girl, if your virtue was ever in danger, it most certainly wasn't then!

The door opened. It was Mélie, making a discreet entrance. I think she has high hopes of Marcel; she sees in him the 'young man' I've hitherto lacked. She brought my little lamp, closed the shutters, drew the curtains and left us in a warm twilight glow. But Marcel had leapt to his feet.

'The lamp! Claudine, whatever time is it?'

'Half past five.'

'Goodness, Grandmother will flay me! I must go – I promised to be back at five.'

'But I thought Aunt Coeur let you have your own sweet way in everything?'

'Yes and no. She's awfully nice but she fusses too much. If I'm back half an hour late, I find her in tears. No joke, I can tell you! And, every time I go out, I have to put up with endless admonitions. "*Do* take care! I nearly die of anxiety when you're out! Whatever you do, don't go through the Rue Cardinet, it's so deserted. Nor by the Étoile, all those carriages when it's getting dark!" And so on and so on. *You've* no idea what it's like, being brought up in cotton-wool! Claudine, come close, whisper . . . You *will* keep the rest of the story for me, won't you? I *can* trust you, can't I?'

'As much as I can trust you,' I said gravely.

'Wicked girl! Give me your paw to kiss. Don't be unkind to your "nephew" any more – he's awfully fond of you. Good-bye, Claudine – see you soon, Claudine!'

From the doorway, he blew me a kiss from the tips of his fingers, just to tease, and fled with his noiseless steps. It had been a wonderful afternoon! My brain was still on fire from it.

'Come on, Fanchette! A little gym! Come and give your future children a bit of exercise!'

SEVEN

MY GAIETY DIDN'T last. I had a sudden relapse into homesickness for Fresnois and the old school. And why? All because of Bérillon; because of that idiot of a Bérillon, that moron of a Bérillon. I'd been dusting books in my little desk, the ones I'd piously brought back from school, and I mechanically opened *The Good Country Housewife, Simple notions of rural and domestic economy for use in girls' schools,* by Louis-Eugène Bérillon. This ineffable little book was a source of pure joy to all the big girls in the school (by that time we hadn't any too many pure joys left) and that great gawk Anaïs and I used to repeat passages aloud over and over again without getting tired of them. On wet days, when we couldn't play marbles or 'He', we used to walk round the new covered-in part of the square playground and put each other posers out of *The Good Housewife*.

'Anaïs, tell me about the *Good Country Housewife* and her ingenuity in the matter of cesspools.'

With her little finger in the air and her flat mouth compressed into an inimitable grimace, Anaïs would recite with a solemnity that made me die of laughter:

'In a sequestered spot on the north side of the garden, the good housewife has persuaded her husband to construct, or has constructed herself, with aid of a few poles, a few planks, and some handfuls of broom or rye-straw, a kind of cabin which serves as a convenience.' (It runs exactly as I'm telling you . . .) 'This cabin, literally hidden under verdure and the flowers of creepers and climbing plants bears far more

46

semblance to a charming bower of greenery than to a latrine.'

'Charming! What truly poetic conception and style! Ah, could I only wander in dreamy meditation to that flowery, perfumed arbour and seat myself there for a moment! . . . But let us pass to the practical side. Kindly proceed, Anaïs.'

'As the excrement of five or six persons in the course of one year is amply sufficient to manure one hectare of ground and that nothing in the nature of . . .'

'Ssh, ssh, don't dwell on it!'

' . . . In the nature of dung ought to be wasted, the cesspool is either a hole dug in the earth and lined with puddled clay or a kind of deep terracotta vessel or, quite simply, an old disused wine-vat.'

'Farewell, ye vats, the vintages are o'er! My dear child, that is perfect. I shall teach you nothing you do not already know by telling you that it is an excellent idea to mix human dung *very thoroughly* with twice its volume of earth and that five kilos are sufficient to manure one *are*[1] and to make two stink. As a reward for your diligence, I authorize you to kiss Dr Dutertre, the District Superintendent, five times.'

'You're joking,' Anaïs murmured dreamily, 'but, if it only needed your permission . . .'

Oh Bérillon, how you've amused those smutty little girls, of whom I was one! We used to mine your preface as we declaimed it. Marie Belhomme, that guileless soul, used to raise her 'midwife's hands' to heaven, as, throbbing with heartfelt conviction, she apostrophized the young peasant girl:

'Unhappy child! How great is your error! Ah, in your own interests and for your own happiness, thrust back as detestable the thought of thus leaving your parents and the cottage where you were born! If you knew at what price those, whose luxury you envy, had bought the silk and the jewels with which they deck themselves out!'

'Ten francs a night,' broke in Anaï. 'I believe that's the price in Paris!'

It was that sour old Bérillon and his worn binding, with the

---

1. 100 square metres.

47

end-papers adorned with transfers, that brought the school the school and my little classmates all too vividly back to my mind. Suddenly, I decided to write to Luce. It was a very long time since I'd had news of her; had she perhaps left Montigny?

Nothing amusing, these last few days, I've been out on foot; I've bestirred myself over the question of dresses and hats. A gentleman followed me. I had the unfortunate idea of putting out a pointed tongue at him. At which he exclaimed eagerly: 'Oh! Give it me!' That will teach me. The prospect of dispensing tea at Aunt Coeur's? 'Bouac!' as that gawk Anaïs used to say – she was marvellous at imitating people being sick. Luckily, Marcel will be there. . . . All the same, I'd infinitely rather drudge away here, even at something boring.

EIGHT

On my next visit to Aunt Coeur, I wore my simple little blue
cloth dress; I hadn't any other suitable ones yet. And besides,
if I 'put on weight', as I probably shall, the ones I ordered too
soon might burst. (Can you see that avalanche of flesh which
would overflow its bounds?) Meanwhile I only weight fifty
kilos[1] on the automatic scales in the Place Saint-Germain-des-
Prés.

I arrived at half past four. There was no one in the drawing-
room yet, except Marcel who was fluttering about noiselessly.
He looked a little pale and there were mauve shadows under
his eyes. I think this slightly tired look made him even more
attractive. He was arranging flowers in vases and humming
under his breath.

'Dear "nephew", why don't you put on a little white
embroidered apron?'

'And would *you* like my trousers?'

'Thanks, I've got some on already. Clumsy! Just look what
you're doing! You're putting the little stand upsi-daisy.'

'Upsi-what?' he said, and burst out laughing.

'Upside down. Isn't there anything you understand?
Wherever were you brought up?'

'Here, alas! Claudine, why don't you wear tailored coats
and skirts? They'd suit you marvellously.'

'Because there isn't a tailor in Montigny.'

'But there are plenty in Paris. Would you like me to take

1. 7 stone 4 lb.

49

you to one? Not to one of the big ones, don't be frightened. Do let's go. I adore anything to do with clothes and fiddling with materials.'

'Yes, I'd love to. Who's going to come here today? They'll all be popping their eyes out at me – Suppose I go away?'

'Not worth it. There won't be masses of people to pop – to stare at you! Madame Barmann, for certain, the old tortoise. Possibly . . . Charlie,' he said, averting his eyes, 'but perhaps he mayn't come. Madame Van Langendonck . . .'

'A Belgian?'

'No, she's a Cypriot.'

'What's the point of being Greek if you go and rig yourself up with a name like that? If I were Flemish, it wouldn't occur to me to call myself Nausicaa!'

'Don't blame *me*! *I* can't do anything about it! Then there'll be some young people who belong to the Barmann set – an old lady Mamma's very fond of and who's always called Madame Amélie – no one knows her surname any more. In fact, hardly anyone . . .'

'Fine. I'm delighted to hear it.'

'Claudine . . . What about Luce?'

'Hush, for goodness' sake! Here's Aunt.'

His grandmother was indeed making her entrance, all in rustling silk.

'Ah! My pretty niece! Have you told them to come and fetch you or would you like Marcel to take you home?'

'But, Aunt, I don't need anyone. I came all by myself.'

She turned purple under her powder.

'Alone! On foot? In a cab?'

'No, Aunt. In the Panthéon-Courcelles bus.'

'Heavens! Heaven! How disgraceful of Claude!'

She did not dare say more. Marcel was watching me sideways and biting his tongue, the wretch. If I laughed, all was lost. He switched on the electric lights and Aunt Coeur emerged from her consternation with a deep sigh.

'Children, I shall have very few friends this week.'

Trrrrr . . . Well, here was one at least. A female one. Hurriedly, I took cover behind the tea-table, and Marcel laughed outright. A humpbacked ball, haloed in iodized

50

cotton-wool screwed into ringlets, had rolled up to Aunt Coeur. Madame Barmann's ample form had been coaxed into a sable coat, much too hot for the time of year and she was perspiring under it. On her head was an owl with outstretched wings. Owl above, owl below. The hooked nose, streaked with broken veins, was not lacking in authority and the grey eyes looked like marbles and rolled alarmingly.

'I'm dead beat. I've done eleven miles on foot,' announced her harsh voice. 'But I've found some wonderful bits of furniture at two old maids' who live in Montrouge. A real expedition! Huysmans would have adored that oddly picturesque jumble of tumble-down houses! I'm hunting all over the place to furnish and decorate our illustrious friend Gréveuille's new house – he has a childlike confidence in me. And, in three weeks' time, one of the shows from La Foire repertory is being done at my house . . . I don't ask you, dear Madame Coeur, to bring that child with you . . .'

She looked at Marcel, and then looked at me, without saying another word.

'My niece Claudine,' Aunt Coeur hastened to introduce me. 'Only just arrived in Paris,' she added, beckoning me to come forward, for, to tell the truth, I was in no hurry to move.

From close to, the 'illustrious friend's' furnisher stared at me with such insolence that I was in two minds whether I wouldn't suddenly lash out at her broken veins with my fist. But at last she transferred her gaze back to Aunt Coeur.

'Charming,' she said roughly. 'Will you bring her to me on Wednesday? Wednesdays are, as you know, innocuous.'

Aunt Coeur thanked her on my behalf. I didn't unclench my teeth and I trembled so violently as I poured out some tea for the impudent old owl that Marcel was exultant. His eyes sparkled with mockery. He whispered to me:

'Claudine, what are we going to do with you if you throw yourself at people's heads like this? Now, now, restrain this uncontrolled expansiveness a little!'

'Go to blazes1' I muttered furiously. 'I can't stand being glared at like that!'

And I went off to my cup of tea, followed by Marcel, much more gracious and girlish than myself, bearing the sandwiches.

Trrrrr . . . Yet another lady. But charming, this one, with eyes right up to her temples and hair right down to her eyes.

'Madame Van Langendonck,' Marcel informed me in a whisper. 'That one who's a Cypriot ! . .'

'As her name indicates, exactly.'

'Does she appeal to you at all, Claudine?'

'She certainly does. She looks like an antelope out on a spree.'

The pretty creature! Flying hair, a vast feathered hat tipped forward, rapturous, short-sighted eyes, a frequent soft, all-embracing gesture with her little right hand that glittered with rings. She was approbation incarnate. To Aunt Coeur and Madam Barmann, she said: 'Yes,' she said: 'You're right,' she said: 'How true that is.' She obviously had a conciliatory nature. Her desire to agree with everyone occasionally landed her in certain inconsistencies. She informed us, practically in the same breath: 'Yesterday at five, I was shopping in the Bon Marché' and 'Yesterday at five, I was at such an interesting lecture'. This did not seem to embarrass anyone, herself least of all.

Aunt Coeur called me over:

'Claudine!'

I went, with a good grace, and smiled at the enchanting face presented to me. Promptly, a wild deluge of compliments poured down on my innocent head.

'Isn't she charming! And such an original type! And what a pretty figure! Seventeen? I should have thought she was at least eighteen . . .'

'Oh no, that's absurd!' protested the owl Barmann. 'She looks much younger than her age.'

'Yes, doesn't she? Hardly fifteen.'

And so the nonsense went on! Marcel's mock solemnity was beginning to get too much for me, when *trrrrr* . . . a gentleman this time. A tall slim gentleman, an attractive gentleman. He had a dark complexion, a great deal of golden-brown hair that was turning white, young eyes with tired eyelids, and a well-groomed moustache, fair, but streaked with silver. He came in, almost as if this were his own home, kissed Aunt Coeur's hand and, standing under the cruel glare of the chandelier, observed mockingly:

'How it rests one's eyes, the gentle twilight of these modern flats!'

Amused at the joke, I looked at Marcel: he wasn't laughing at all and was contemplating the gentleman in an anything but benevolent way.

'Who's that?'

'It's my father,' he answered icily, going up to the gentleman who shook his hand pleasantly and absent-mindedly as one pulls one's gun-dog's ear.

His father! I didn't think it at all funny! I must have looked a perfect idiot. A father with whom he'd been at loggerheads, that was obvious. His son only resembled him very vaguely. The obstinate arch of the eyebrows, perhaps? But all Marcel's features were so refined that one still couldn't be quite sure. What a funny expression, at once cold and submissive, my nephew had put on for the author of his being! In any case, he certainly hadn't proclaimed from the roof-tops that he had a Papa; yet this one seemed to me a father anyone would positively flaunt. But, evidently, with both of them, the call of the blood didn't sound loud enough in their ears to deafen them.

'Things going all right with you, my boy? Working well?'

'Yes, Father.'

'You look a little tired to me.'

'Oh no, Father.'

'You ought to have come to the races with me today. That would have shaken you up.'

'Father, I absolutely had to hand round the tea.'

'That's true. You absolutely had to hand round the tea. Heaven forbid I should seduce you from such serious duties!'

As the Barmann owl and the Cypriot antelope were deep in conversation, the one authoritative and the other so compliant that her soft agreement blunted every barb, Aunt Coeur risked, less unctuously than usual:

'Renaud, do you really think a racecourse quite the right place for that child?

'Why not, Madame? He'd see some very eligible people . . .

and even more Israelites,' he added softly with a sidelong glance at Madame Barmann.

This was absolutely splendid! I was simmering with suppressed joy. If this went on, the English porcelain I was reverently handling would soon be strewing the carpet. Aunt Coeur lowered her eyes and blushed imperceptibly. No doubt about it, he wasn't at all polite but I was thoroughly enjoying myself. (Oh! 'Not half having fun, I wasn't!' as Luce would have said.) Marcel was counting the flowers on the velvet upholstery with the expression of a girl who hadn't been asked to dance.

'You betted at the races no doubt,' my aunt inquired sadly, with a face of despair.

The gentleman gave a melancholy shake of his head.

'I even went so far as to lose. So I gave twenty francs to the cabby who drove me back.'

'Why?' asked his son, raising his eyebrows.

'Because, with what I'd lost, that made it up to a round sum.'

'Hpppp . . .' This was that idiot of a Claudine exploding into a giggle. My cousin . . . (let me see, if he was the father of my nephew, was he my cousin? I was all at sea) . . . my cousin turned his head towards that indecorous laugh.

'Do you know my little niece Claudine, Renaud? My brother Claude's daughter, only just arrived in Paris. She and Marcel are the best of friends in the world already.'

'I'm anything but sorry for Marcel,' declared the gentleman to whom I had offered my hand.

He had only looked at me for a second, but he was someone who knew how to look. A zigzagging look, with an imperceptible pause at the hair, the eyes, the lower part of the face and the hands. Marcel moved away to the tea-table and I prepared to follow him . . .

'Claude's daughter . . .' my cousin racked his brains. 'Oh! wait a minute, I've so little sense of genealogies . . . But, in that case, Mademoiselle is Marcel's aunt? But this situation is pure vaudeville, isn't it . . . *Cousin?*'

'Yes, Uncle,' I said without hesitation.

'What luck! That'll make me two babies to take to the

Circus if your father permits me to . . . you're how old . . . fifteen, sixteen?'

I corrected him, offended.

'Over seventeen!'

'Seventeen . . . yes, those eyes. Marcel, that makes a change for you, eh? – having a girl friend?'

'Oh,' I said laughing, 'I'm must too much of a boy for him!'

My cousin Uncle, who had followed us to the tea-table, scrutinized me sharply, but I looked such a good little girl!

'Too much of a boy for him? No, definitely not,' he said, with a touch of mockery in his voice.

Marcel fidgeted so clumsily with a little enamel spoon that he managed to twist its handle. He shrugged his graceful shoulders and walked out of the room, with his charming, quiet step, shutting the dining-room door behind him. Old Mother Barmann went off, throwing me a highly absurd 'Good-bye, little one!' On her way out, she passed a new arrival. This was an old lady with white hair done in bandeaux, looking exactly like dozens of other old ladies, who sat down in two movements and refused tea. What luck!

My cousin Uncle, who had accompanied the owl to the door, returned to the tea-table and asked me for some tea. He demanded cream and, furthermore, two lumps of sugar, also a sandwich, not the top one because it must have got dry, and various other things. But he had the same type of greediness as I had and I didn't get impatient. I found him sympathetic, this cousin Uncle. I was longing to know what was wrong between him and Marcel. He looked as if he were thinking about it himself, and, while still munching a delicious little shortbread biscuit, he asked me in a muffled voice:

'Has my son talked to you about me?'

Misery me! What could I do? What could I say? I dropped my spoon to give myself time, just as I used to drop my penholder at school, and, at last, I replied:

'No – at least I don't remember it.'

It wasn't a very brilliant effort but it was all I could manage. He didn't look surprised. He went on eating. He wasn't old. He was a father who was still young. His nose amused me; it was slightly aquiline, with mobile nostrils. Under very black lashes, his eyes gleamed dark blue-grey. For a man, his ears weren't ugly. His hair was going white at the temples and fluffed out. At Montigny there was a beautiful silvery dog who had fur just that colour. Without warning, he raised his eyes so suddenly that he caught me looking at him.

'Do you think I'm ugly?'

'No, Uncle, not in the least.'

'Not as handsome as Marcel, eh?'

'Ah, no certainly not! There doesn't exist another boy as pretty as he is. And there can only be very few women who can hold a candle to him.'

'Perfectly true! My paternal pride is flattered. My son isn't exactly forthcoming, though, is he?'

'Oh yes, he *is*! He came to see me at home yesterday, all on his own, and we talked away like anything. He's much better brought up than I am.'

'Much better than I am, too. But you astonish me by saying he's already paid you a visit. You positively astound me. It's a conquest. I'd like to meet . . . I mean, it would give me great pleasure if you would introduce me to your revered father, Cousin. The Family! First and foremost, I am the most devout upholder of the Family. I am a pillar of tradition.'

'And of the turf!'

'Oh! but it really *is* true – that you're shockingly brought up! When can I find your father at home?'

'In the morning, he never goes out. In the afternoon, he goes and sees people who have decorations and stirs up dust in libraries. But not every single day. Anyway, if you really want to come, I'll tell him to stay in. He's still fairly obedient to me about little things.'

'Ah, little things! They're the only ones that matter: they take up all the room and there's none left for the big ones. Let's see now . . . what have you seen in Paris up to now?'

'The Luxembourg and the big shops.'

'Quite sufficient, in short. Suppose I took you to a concert on Sunday, with Marcel? I think the concerts are "exclusive" enough this year for my son to consent to risk being seen at them occasionally.'

'The big concerts? Oh, yes . . . thank you. I've been longing to go to them, though I don't know much about them. I've so seldom heard good orchestras.'

'Good, that's settled. What else? You strike me as a young person who's not difficult to entertain. Dear me, I should like to have had a daughter – I'd have brought her up so well in my own way! What sort of things do you like?'

I lit up.

'Heaps of things! Rotten bananas, chocolates, lime buds, the inside of the tails of artichokes, the "cuckoo" on fruit-trees . . .' (I didn't stop to explain that 'cuckoo' is our name at home for the gum) 'new books, and penknives with lots of blades, and . . .'

Out of breath, I burst out laughing because my cousin Uncle had solemnly taken a notebook out of his pocket and was writing in it:

'A moment's respite, I implore you, dear child! Chocolates, rotten bananas – horror! – inside of artichokes, that's child's play. But, as for lime buds and the cuckoo that perches exclusively on fruit-trees, I don't know any retail-houses in Paris. Can one write direct to the manufacturers?'

What luck! Here was a man who really knew how to amuse children! Why did his son look as if he didn't get on with him? At that very moment, Marcel returned, wearing a much too indifferent expression on his charming mug. My cousin Uncle stood up, the white-haired old lady stood up, the pretty Cypriot Van Langendonck stood up: general retreat. When these ladies had gone, my aunt inquired:

'Darling, now who's going to take you home to your father? Would you like my maid to?'

'Or why not me, Grandmother?' Marcel suggested charmingly.

'You? . . . Very well, but take a cab by the hour, my pet.'

'What, you let him go out in a cab at this hour?' exclaimed my cousin Uncle, so sarcastically that Aunt Coeur noticed it.

'My friend, I'm responsible for his welfare. Who else takes any trouble over this child?'

I did not hear what followed: I went to put my hat and coat on. When I returned, my cousin Uncle had disappeared and

Aunt Coeur was very gradually resuming her smile of an old lady who has lodged in the Tuileries.

Good-byes, 'see you soons', then the cold street after the shut-in warmth of the drawing-room.

We got into a pneumatic-tyred cab on the rank in the Rue Joffroy! The joy of pneumatic tyres hasn't begun to pall on me yet and I admitted it. Marcel smiled, but said nothing. Suddenly, I attacked.

'He's charming, your father.'

'Charming.'

'Restrain your delirious tenderness, most passionate of sons!'

'What do you expect me to say? I haven't just discovered Papa for the first time today, have I? I've known him for seventeen years.'

I shut myself up in wounded discretion.

'Don't sulk, Claudine . . . it's all too complicated to explain.'

'You're quite right, my friend. It's nothing whatever to do with me. If you don't make a great fuss of your father, you must have your reasons.'

'Most certainly I have. He made Mamma very unhappy.'

'For long?'

'Yes . . . for eighteen months.'

'Did he beat her?'

'No, of course not! But he was never at home.'

'And you? Has he made you very unhappy?'

'Oh, it's not that. But,' my 'nephew' explained with controlled fury, 'he can be so biting! Our two natures don't harmonize in any way.'

He threw out these last words in a disillusioned, theatrical voice that inwardly convulsed me.

'Claudine! The other day, we stopped just at Luce's letter. Do go on from there, please! It's far more interesting than a lot of domestic quarrels and dirty family linen!'

Ah, I'd found *my* Marcel, my pretty Marcel, again. Under the passing gas-lamps, his slender face shone out and disappeared, shone out again and vanished, and, every three seconds, I could make out the dimple in his delicate darkness,

58

from the new faces and the over-strong tea, I snuggled my cold hands comfortably into my 'nephew's' feverishly hot ones. Up to now I'd told him the truth; today it was a question of inventions, something really impressive. I'd got to lie! 'Lie like a trooper,' as Mélie says.

'Well, then I gave Luce back her "minced" letter.'

'Torn up?'

'Yes. Minced into little bits.'

'What did she say?'

'She cried without any shame . . . out loud.'

'And . . . was that your last word?'

Ambiguous, and, as it were, slightly shamed silence on the part of Claudine . . . Marcel thrust his pretty head forward avidly.

'No . . . She did everything she could to make me yield. When I was "on water" . . . you see, we used to carry up water in turn . . . she waited for me in the dormitory till the others had gone down so that she could speak to me. She threatened to weep out loud to annoy me and I got so fed up that I ended up by sitting down on the bed and taking her on my lap. She clasped her little hands behind her neck, hid her face on my shoulder and pointed out the boys' dormitory opposite, over at the end of the playground, where you could see them undressing at night . . .'

'You could see them un . . .?'

'Yes, and they used to make signs. Luce laughed very softly into my neck and beat my legs with her heels. I told her: "Get up . . . *Cave* . . . Mademoiselle's coming!" But she suddenly flung herself on me and began to kiss me wildly . . .'

'Wildly . . .' Marcel repeated like an echo and his hands slowly turned cold in mine.

'So then I promptly jumped to my feet and nearly knocked her down. She cried out, very low: "You're wicked . . . you're wicked! Heartless!"'

'And then?'

'And then I gave her such a real good thrashing that her arms were all blue and her scalp tingling. I can hit jolly hard when I try. She adored that. She hid her face and let herself be beaten, letting out great sighs . . . (The bridges,

Marcel, we're nearly there.) Great sighs . . . just like you're doing now.'

'Claudine,' said his soft, slightly choked voice, 'won't you go on and tell me some more? I . . . I simply love these stores.'

'So I observe . . . Only, you know the conditions?'

'Ssh . . . I know the conditions. Give and take. But,' he said, putting his face, with its pink dry mouth and eyes that had grown enormous, quite close to mine, 'friendships that are passionate, but chaste and entirely of the heart, are more difficult to tell about. I'm afraid of being meagre, as well as clumsy.'

'Take care, you're being tempted to tell lies. I shall seal my lips.'

'No, no! I shall compel you to talk now! We're there. I'll get out and ring the bell.'

When the door was opened, he took my hands again in his moist fingers, squeezed them much too hard and kissed them one after the other.

'My compliments to my uncle, Claudine. And my respects to Fanchette. Claudine, you wonderful, surprising girl! How could I ever have expected all this pleasure would come to me from Montigny?'

That was really quite well said.

At the dinner-table, my nerves became a little calmer as I told Papa (who didn't listen) all about my afternoon and my cousin Uncle. Fanchette, the darling, ran her nose along the hem of my skirt to find out where I'd been. She now had a pretty round belly which she carried gaily and which did not prevent her from leaping after the moths round the lamp. It was no use my telling her: 'Fanchette, one shouldn't stretch one's arms up when one's pregnant'; she didn't pay any attention.

As we were eating the Cheshire cheese, Papa, no doubt suddenly inspired by the Holy Spirit, emitted a loud cry.

'What is it, Papa? A new slug?'

'I've got it, I know who he is! All that business had gone clean out of my mind. When one's entire life is occupied with serious things, trifles like that get forgotten. Poor Ida, Marcel, Renaud . . . I've got it now. Six and thirty swine! Wilhelmine's

60

daughter married this Renaud when she was very young and he wasn't very old either. She bored him, I think. Just fancy . . . a daughter of Wilhelmine's! . . . Well, then she had a son – Marcel. They didn't get along any too well, after the child. A touchy, Puritanical little woman. She said: "I'm going home to mother." He said: I'll get them to call a cab for you." Soon after, she died of something or other rapid. There!'

That night, before I went to bed, I said to Mélie, as she was closing the shutters:

'Mélie, I now possess an uncle. No, I mean I've a cousin and a nephew, you understand!'

'You've also got maggots in your brain, at this moment. And look at that cat, now. Ever since she's been in the family way she's always in the drawers and cupboards, a-moithering of everything.'

'You must put out a basket for her. Will it be soon?'

'Not for another fortnight.'

'But I haven't brought her basket of hay.'

'That's a pity. Never mind. I'll buy her a dog-basket with a cushion.'

'She won't have anything to do with it. It's too Parisian for her.'

'Go on with you! What about the tom from downstairs? *He* wasn't too Parisian for her, was he?'

NINE

AUNT WILHELMINE CAME to see me but I wasn't in. She talked to Papa, Mélie told me, and was 'in ever such a state' to find I'd gone out alone. (No doubt she's aware that our neighbourhood is infested with students from the Beaux Arts Art School.)

I had gone out-of-doors to see some leaves.

Alas! green leaves! they come out early here!

There, at the very most, the hawthorn hedges would be veiled, at long intervals, with that green haze their tiny tender leaves weave for them and that seems to hang from their twigs. In the Luxembourg, I wanted to eat young tree-shoots as I used to at Montigny, but here they're covered with coal-dust and scrunch under your teeth. And never, never once did I breathe the dank smell of rotting leaves and reedy ponds, nor the faintly acrid tang of wind that has blown over woods where charcoal is burning. *There* the first violets would be out, I could see them! The border near the garden wall that faces west would be flowering with little violets – ugly, puny and stunted, but with a heavenly smell.

How miserable I am! The excessive warmth of this Paris spring and its mugginess make me feel like nothing so much as a wretched wild animal condemned to live in the zoo. They sell primroses and yellow daisies and daffodils by barrow-loads here. But the daisy-balls I make from force of habit don't amuse anyone but Fanchette who has stayed nimble, in spite of her taut little corporation, and handles them deftly, using her paw like a spoon. I am in a thoroughly bad state of mind . . . Luckily my body is all right: I frequently verify this as I squat in the hot water of my tub and it gives me considerable satisfaction. It's long-limbed and supple and elastic, not very plump, but muscular enough not to seem too thin.

I've kept myself supple, even though I've no longer a tree to climb. One of my efforts was to balance myself in my tub on my right foot and bend back as far as possible with my left leg raised very high, my right arm used as a balancing-pole and my left hand under the nape of my neck. It sounds nothing – but you just try! Flop! Over I went backwards. And, as I hadn't dried myself, my behind made a round wet patch on the floor. (Fanchette, sitting on the bed, stared at me with cold contempt both for my clumsiness and for this unaccountable mania of mine for sitting in water.) But I do other exercises with brilliant success; putting my feet alternatively on the nape of my neck or bending back till my head if on a level with my calves. Mélie is full of admiration, but warns me against too much of these gymnastics.

'You'll go and split yourself one of these days!'

After all these intimate diversions, I collapse again into apathy or irritability: and my hands too hot or too cold; my eyes languid and over-bright; prickly and edgy all over. I don't say my cross cat's face is ugly, actually it's the reverse, with its cap of curly hair. The one thing I lack, the one thing I need . . . I shall discover it only too soon. And, besides, it would be humiliating . . .

Up to now, the net result of all this for Claudine has been an unexpected passion for Francis Jammes because that odd poet understands the country and animals and old-fashioned gardens and the importance of the stupid little things in life.

TEN

MY COUSIN UNCLE came to see Papa this morning. At first
Papa was furious at being disturbed, but he promptly became
quite human because this man Renaud knows how to be
charming and disarming. In broad daylight, he had more
white hairs but his face looked younger than when I saw it
first and his eyes were an unusual, highly individual slate-
colour. He got Papa launched on malacology and my noble
father was inexhaustible on the subject. Appalled by this spate
of words, I stemmed it by saying: 'Papa, I want to let my uncle
see Fanchette.'

And I carried my uncle off to my room, enchanted to see
that he appreciated the little four-poster and the old-
fashioned chintz and my beloved, shabby little desk. He deftly
massaged and scratched Fanchette's sensitive stomach and
cleverly talked cat-language to her. Whatever Marcel says
about him, he's *definitely* 'all right!'

'My dear child, a white cat and a tub-armchair are indispensable objects in a young girl's room. All that's missing is
the nice, suitable novel . . . no, here it is. Good Lord, it's
André Tourette. What an extraordinary notion!'

'Oh, you'll see plenty of others! You'll have to get used to
them. I read everything.

'Everything? Saying a good deal, isn't it? Don't try and
shock me . . . that's just ridiculous.'

'Ridiculous!' I said, choking with rage. 'I'm quite old
enough to reach what I choose.'

'Dear, dear, dear! Certainly your father – incidentally, he's charming – is no ordinary father but . . . well, well, there are some things you'd be none the worse for not knowing. My dear . . .' he added, seeing I was nearly in tears. 'I don't want to hurt your feelings. Whatever's come over me to moralize like this? I'm being preternaturally avuncular. Which doesn't prevent *you* from being the prettiest and most delicious of nieces, bibliomania apart. And you're going to give me your little paw in token of peace.'

I gave it him. But I suddenly felt miserable. I had been so determined to find that man charming in every possible way.

He kissed my hand. He was the second man who had kissed my hand. And I noticed the difference. Marcel's kiss is the faintest brush, so light and hasty that I don't know whether a pair of lips or a hurried finger has touched my skin. But when it came to his father, I had time to feel the shape of his mouth.

He has gone. He will come back on Sunday to fetch me for the concert. He has gone . . .

I ask you! An uncle who didn't look in the least the old-fashioned kind! Do *I* nag *him* about his habit of losing his money at the races? He might, quite naturally, reply that he was no longer seventeen and that his name was not Claudine.

And, as if all that weren't enough, I still have no news from Luce.

Claudine is playing at being a fashionable lady. Claudine is ordering herself dress after dress and tormenting the ancient and superannuated Poullanx, dressmaker, as well as Madame Abraham Lévi, milliner. My uncle has assured me that, in Paris, all the milliners are Jewesses. This one, though she's on the Left Bank, displays a liveliness of taste that is rare and refreshing; besides, it amuses her to find hats for my pointed face and short, bushy hair. Before trying them on, she brushes my hair forward roughly, fluffs up the sides, takes two steps backwards and says rapturously: 'There! Now you look exactly like Polaire!' Personally, I'd rather look like Claudine. As, from February onwards, the women here plant greenery on their heads, I've chosen two summer hats; a big black crinoline straw with feathers 'makes you look like a millionaire's baby', Madame Lévi declared, pouting amiably into her dark moustache – and another one, russet, trimmed with black velvet. They've got to go with everything. *I* don't share that gawk Anaïs's tastes. She was never happy unless her head was capsizing under three kilogrammes of roses.

And I'm working out still another blue dress. I cultivate blue, not for its own sake, but for the way it sets off the Spanish-tobacco colour of my eyes.

No sign of Marcel. I feel vaguely that he's sulking with me. 'Sulking' is too strong a word, but I can sense a muffled resentment. Today, as it's raining, I'm consoling myself with old and new books, with Balzacs I've read over and over again, that have crumbs of long-ago meals hidden between their pages . . . there's a cake-crumb that comes from Montigny – smell, Fanchette! Heartless beast, it didn't mean a thing to her; she was listening to the noises of saucepans in the kitchen! . . . Papa, his tie looking like a shoestring, pats my head whenever he passes through. How happy that man is in having found the rich fulfilment of life and a fruitful new channel for his energies in slugs . . . who is going to take place of the slug for *me*?

A letter. Why, yes, it was from Claire!

Darling, I've got blissful news to tell you. I'm being married in a month's time to my dear beloved whose photograph I sent you. He is richer than I am; he has no troubles, but that doesn't matter. I'm so happy! He's going to be manager of a factory in Mexico (!!!) and I shall go out there with him. Now you can see life really is like it is in novels. You used to laugh at me in the old days when I told you so. I so much want you to come to my wedding, etc., etc., etc.

After that came endless repetitions and all the chatter of a little girl delirious with happiness. She deserves all her joy, that gentle, trusting child – and such a nice decent child, too! That trust and that gentleness, by a miraculous chance, have protected her better than the most knowing artfulness. This wasn't entirely due to her, but it has certainly been the case. I answered her straight away in a letter full of nice, affectionate nothings. And then I stayed sitting there by a little wood fire – shivery, as always, the moment it rains – waiting for night and dinner-time, in a shaming state of misery and dejection.

She was getting married; *she* was seventeen. And I? . . . Oh, if I could only be given back Montigny, and last year, and the year before that, and my turbulent, indiscreet prying into other people's affairs! If I only could have back my disappointed love for Mademoiselle's little Aimée and my sensual bullying of Luce – for I've no one here and don't even want to behave badly!

Whoever would have believed that she was revolving such tearful thoughts, this Claudine, squatting cross-legged in a dressing-gown before the marble chimneypiece and apparently completely absorbed in roasting one side of a bar of chocolate kept upright between a pair of tongs? When the surface exposed to the fire softened, blackened, crackled, and blistered, I lifted it off in thin layers with my little knife . . . Exquisite taste, a mixture of grilled almonds and grated vanilla! The melancholy sweetness of savouring the toasted chocolate and, at the same time, staining one's toenails pink with a little rage soaked in Papa's red ink!

The returning sun showed me the absurdity of my desolation of last night. All the more so because Marcel arrived at half past five, lively and beautiful as . . . as only Marcel can be. His pongee tie was a dull turquoise that brightened his lips to China rose, an artificial rose like a made-up mouth. Heavens, that little furrow between the nose and the upper lip and the imperceptible down that silvered it! Pure silk velvet at 15 francs 90 a yard wasn't as smooth.

'Nephew, how pleased I am to see you! You're not shocked that I've kept my little apron on?'

'It's charming, your little apron. Keep it on, you make me think (what already!) of Montigny.'

'I don't need to keep it on to make *me* think of Montigny. If you knew how that hurts sometimes!'

'Oh come now, none of that nostalgic nonsense, Claudine! It doesn't suit you a bit!'

His levity was cruel to me at that moment and, no doubt, I gave him a nasty look, for he became tractable and charming.

'Wait a moment. Homesickness! I'm going to breathe on your eyes and it will fly away!

With his woman's grace, a compound of ease and of extraordinary precision of movement, he caught me round the waist and gently breathed on my half-closed eyes. He kept the game up and finally declared, 'You smell of . . . cinnamon, Claudine.'

'Why cinnamon?' I asked languidly, leaning against his arm and half tranced by his light breath.

'I don't know. A warm smell, a smell like some exotic sweetmeat.'

'So that's it! An oriental bazaar, in fact?'

'No. A bit like Viennese pastry – a smell good to eat. And what do *I* smell of?' he demanded, putting his velvety cheek very close to my mouth.

'New-mown hay,' I said, sniffing it. And, as his cheek did not withdraw, I kissed it gently, without pressing. But I would have kissed a bunch of flowers or a ripe peach in just the same way. There are some scents one can only take in properly with one's mouth.

Marcel understood that, it seemed. He did not return my kiss, but drawing back, he said, with an absurd little pout:

'Hay? That's a very artless smell. . . . By the way, are you coming to the concert tomorrow?'

'Certainly. Your father came to see Papa the other morning, didn't you know?'

'No,' he said with indifference. 'I don't see Papa every day. He hasn't time. And now I must be off, I've only got a minute. Do you know, you ungrateful little girl, whom I'm keeping waiting by staying here? Charlie!'

He burst into a mischievous laugh and fled.

But I fully appreciated the costliness of this favour.

ELEVEN

'PAPA, I'M GOING to the concert in a moment. Do hurry a little. I'm quite aware that cold fried eggs are a dish for the gods, but all the same, do be quick.'

'Inferior creature!' declaimed Papa, shrugging his shoulders. 'All women are on a level with the least intelligent of she-asses. I am soaring in the realm of ideas!'

'Take care, you'll upset the water-jug with the tip of your wing. Don't you think my dress suits me?'

'Hmm . . . yes. . . . Is it made from one of last year's garments?'

'Certainly not. You paid for it two days ago.'

'No doubt. This household is a bottomless gulf. Is your aunt well?'

'But she came here. Didn't you see her?

'No – yes – I can't remember; she bores me. Her son's a great improvement on her. Very intelligent! Has views on all sorts of things! Even about malacology, he's not too scandalously ignorant.'

'Who do you mean? Marcel?'

'No, no, not the little squit. What's-his-name . . . Wilhelmine's son-in-law, that's the one I mean.'

The little squit, the little squit! So Papa didn't care a rap about little squits like that! Not that I think badly of Marcel's father, who attracts me and warms the cockles of my heart, but *really* . . .

The bell. Mélie made haste slowly to answer it. My cousin Uncle and my 'nephew' entered, both resplendent. Marcel, in particular, in a tight-fitting suit too new for my taste; beside his father, he seemed a little diminished.

'My dear sir . . . How pretty that girl of yours looks in that big black hat!'

'No bad, not bad,' Papa said carelessly, disguising his very genuine admiration.

Marcel examined me critically as usual.

'Do put on suède ones instead of pearl-grey kid; they're prettier with blue.'

He was right. I changed my gloves.

All three of us in a closed cab, Marcel on the torturingly narrow pull-down seat, we bowled along towards the Châtelet. As I was quaking inwardly, I said nothing and behaved well. There was no danger of the conversation between Uncle Renaud and his son becoming over-exciting.

'Do you want to see the programme? Here you are. *The Damnation of Faust*. It's not a first performance . . .'

'It's a first performance for me.'

In the square, the spitting sphinxes of the Palm-tree Fountain reminded me of the disgusting game we used to adore at Montigny: standing in a row, five or six of us horrid little girls would fill our cheeks with water and imitate the sphinxes. The one who spat furthest won a marble or some nuts.

At the box-office and on the staircase, my cousin Uncle kept bowing to people or shaking hands with them. Evidently he came here often.

It was badly lit. It smelt of horse-dung. Why did it smell of horse-dung? I asked Marcel under my breath why and he answered: 'It's because they're playing *Michael Strogoff* every night.' Uncle Renaud installed us in the front row of the dress-circle. Scowling a little at being in such conspicuous seats, I looked round me shyly, but it was difficult to see after coming in from broad daylight, so I felt at my ease. It was all right, there were plenty of ladies! And what a row they were making! All that banging of doors in the boxes, all that pushing about of chairs . . . it was like being in church at Montigny where no one paid any attention to what Father Millet was saying in the pulpit, nor even to the altar.

The Châtalet auditorium was large but ugly and commonplace; the lights showed red in a halo of dust. I can assure you it *did* smell of horse-dung! And all those heads down below – the men's black and the women's beflowered. I wondered, if I threw bread down to those people, whether they'd open their mouths to catch it? When was it going to begin? My cousin Uncle, seeing me pale and nervous, took my hand and kept it between his fingers as a gesture of protection.

A bearded gentleman, with shoulders slightly 'askew', advanced on to the stage and applause (already!) drowned the extremely disagreeable tumult of chatter and of instruments tuning-up. It was Colonne himself. He rapped his desk twice with a little baton, inspected those under his command with an encircling glance, and raised his arm. At the first chords of the *Damnation* a nervous lump rose up from my stomach to my throat and stayed there, nearly choking me. I had hardly ever heard an orchestra and those bows were playing on my nerves. I had a crazy terror of bursting into tears from sheer nervous exasperation and making an utter fool of myself! With tremendous efforts, I mastered this ridiculous feeling and I gently withdrew my hand from my Uncle's so as to get myself under better control.

Marcel was looking round everywhere and making signs with his head towards the gallery where I could make out soft felt hats, long hair, clean-shaven faces, and aggressive moustaches.

'Up there,' explained the Uncle in a whisper, 'are all the people who really matter. Anarchist musicians, writers who will change the face of the world and even extremely nice boys who haven't a penny and love music. It's up there too they put "the man who protests". He whistles and utters his obscure maledictions; a military policeman gathers him like a flower, expels him and lets him return discreetly by another door. Colonne has tried engaging one specially at modest fees, but he's given it up. "The man who protests" must first and foremost have passionate convictions.'

At a certain point, I wanted to laugh. It was when Mephistopheles was singing the song of the flea, to such a burlesque accompaniment that Berlioz must have done it on

71

purpose. Yes, I wanted to laugh because the baritone was obviously finding it tremendously difficult not to *act* what he was singing. He restrained himself as much as he could from being diabolical, but he could feel that forked feather waving above his forehead and his eyebrows shaped themselves of their own accord into the traditional circumflex accent.

Right up to the interval, I listened with all my inexpert ears that had had little practice in distinguishing the tones of the various instruments.

'What is it that's singing in the orchestra, among the wood-wind, Uncle?'

'A bass flute, I'm pretty sure. We'll ask Maugis in the interval, if you like.'

The interval came all too soon, in my opinion. I detest being rationed and having a pleasure cut short without my asking. Where were all those people leaving the auditorium rushing to so fast? Actually, they were only going out into the passages. I glued myself to Marcel's side, but Uncle Renaud authoritatively slipped his own arm under mine.

'Collect yourself, little girl. Even though we're limited to damning Faust today and there won't be any of the latest works from the young men of the new School, I can show you some tolerably well-known faces. And your illusions will strew the ground like flowers from withered garlands!'

'Oh! Is it the music that's inspired you to such eloquence!'

'Yes. The real truth about me is that behind a thinker's brow I have a young girl's soul.' His slate-coloured eyes, indulgent and lazy, smiled at me with a smile that calmed me and gave me confidence. His son, who was rather overdoing being all things to all men, had just gone off to make his bow to Madame Barmann who was dominating and laying down the law in the midst of a group of men.

'Quick, let's escape,' my Uncle implored in alarm. 'She'll go and quote the latest aphorism of her "illustrious friend" at us, once we get dragged into her wake!'

'Which illustrious friend? The one she was talking about at Aunt Coeur's the other Sunday?'

'Gréveuille, a very much sought-after member of the Academy whom she . . . subsidizes, boards, and lodges. Last winter I still used to dine in that set-up and I went off with a slightly embarrassing picture in my mind: the great man installed in front of the Louis XIII chimney-piece and artlessly presenting his two unbuttoned boots to the fire.'

'Why hadn't he buttoned them up?' (I put the question to him with a convincing imitation of innocence.)

'Because, of course, he'd just been . . . Claudine, you're intolerable! Anyway, it's entirely my fault. I'm not used to little girls. I've been an Uncle for such a very short time. But I'll watch my step from now on.'

'What a pity! It won't be nearly so amusing.'

'Ssh, you little horror! As you read *everything*, do you know who Maugis is? I can see him over there.'

'Maugis? Yes, he does music criticism – articles all peppered with puns and vulgarities – a hotpotch of affectation and lyrical enthusiasm that I don't always understand . . .'

' "Affection and lyrical enthusiasm!" Goodness, what an amusing niece I've got! Do you know that's not at all a bad criticism? But I'm positively going to enjoy taking you out, chicken!'

'Thanks very much! If I know what those words really mean, you "took me out" today just out of politeness, didn't you?'

We had come within earshot of the Maugis in question. He was extremely animated and holding forth in a throaty voice that kept choking; he appeared to be in one of his lyrical moods . . . I went up closer still. No doubt he was giving full vent to his admiration? Bumpetty-bump! (as they say at home when a child tumbles down . . .) *This* was what I heard:

'No, but did you hear that swine of a trombone baying among the new-blown roses of that night? If Faust could sleep in spite of the rumpus that ass was making, he must have been reading *Fertility* before he dossed down. Besides, what a dung-heap of an orchestra! In the syphilitic Ballet, there was a putrid little flautist who didn't stick at blowing his confounded nose at the same time the harp were doing their harmonic what-d'you-call-'ems. If I could lay hands on him, I'd stuff his flute up his . . .'

'My friend, my friend,' my Uncle soothingly admonished

the back of the frenzied speaker. 'If you go on, you'll lose all moderation of speech!'

Maugis swung his heavy shoulders round and displayed a short nose, protruding blue eyes under drooping lids and a huge, ferocious moustache above a babyish mouth. Still swelling with righteous fury, his bulging eyes and his congested neck made him look like a slightly froglike little bull. (I have profited by the natural history lessons of Montigny). But he was smiling now, with a disarming mouth, and, as he bowed, revealing a vast pink pate, I noticed that the whole lower part of the face – the nebulous chin vanishing in rolls of fat and the childish lips – incessantly contradicted the energy of the huge forehead and the short, obstinate nose. I was introduced to him. His response was:

'My dear old chap, why do you bring this young person to this dubious resort? It's so delightful in the Tuileries with a nice hoop . . .'

I was offended and said nothing. And my dignity immensely amused the two men.

'Is your Marcel here?' Maugis asked my Uncle.

'Yes. He came with his aunt.'

'*What*!' exclaimed the critic with a start, 'you mean to say that now he's going about openly with his . . .'

'With Claudine,' explained my Uncle, shrugging his shoulders. 'Claudine here is his aunt. We are a complicated family.'

'Ah, Mademoiselle, so you are Marcel's aunt? Interesting irony on the part of fate. Or possibly a happy prognostication.'

'If you think you're being funny . . .' growled my Uncle, torn between wanting to laugh and wanting to scold.

'One does one's poor best,' replied the other.

What was all that about? There was something there that I didn't understand. It wasn't till long after that I discovered that, in slang, 'aunt' meant young men like Charlie.

The pretty Cypriot, Madame Van Langendonck, swept past us, escorted by six men who all seemed to be equally infatuated with her and whom she caressed impartially with her enraptured gazelle's eyes.

74

'What a delicious creature! Don't you think so, Uncle?'

'I certainly do. She's one of those women one simply must invite to at-home-days. She's both decorative and inflammatory.'

'And,' added Maugis, 'while the men are gazing at her, they forgot to gobble up all the stuffed rolls.'

'Who's that you're bowing to, Uncle?'

'An extremely estimable trio.'

'Like the César Franck one,' broke in Maugis.

'Three inseparable friends,' my Uncle went on, 'who are always invited together and everyone would be sorry to leave one out. They're good-looking, they're well-behaved, and, incredible as it may seem, absolutely irreproachable and decent. One composes music, charming, very individual music; the second – the one who's talking to Princess de C- – sings it like a great artist, and the third does extremely clever pastels while he listens to them.'

'If I were a woman,' concluded Maugis, 'I should want to marry all three of them!'

'What are their names?'

'You'll nearly always hear people mention all three together: Baville, Bréda, and della Sugès.'

My Uncle exchanged a few passing words with the trio, who were pleasant to look at. One looked like a Valois who had strayed into our midst from another century, slim and high-bred as a heraldic greyhound; this was Baville. The handsome, healthy boy with shadows under his blue eyes and a delicious feminine mouth was the tenor, Bréda. The tall, casual della Sugès, who retained something of the East in his matt complexion and the marked curve of his nose, watched the people go by, as serious as a well-behaved child.

'You're an expert, Maugis. Point out a few notorious specimens to Claudine.'

'Specimens of the world and his wife? Cert'nly. It's a charming spectacle to present to a female infant . . . Here, young *backfisch*, behold, to begin with . . . honour to whom honour is due . . . the fashionable sterilizer dear to all ladies who never, never more, *ovariemore*, wish to combat the depopulation of our beloved country . . .'

My Uncle could not repress a little gesture of annoyance. He
had no need to: my fat showman talked with such obviously
deliberate volubility that I didn't manage to catch half his
jokes. They got no further than his moustache and I was sorry
because my Uncle's irritation proved they were pretty stiff.

Gradually, Maugis modified his tone somewhat as he
enumerated further celebrities.

'Now, enviable aunt of the enviable Marcel, cast your eyes
on one of the critics whom Sainte-Anne envies us; that beard
– about which we can sing a roundelay, if you like, that it is
gilded with peroxide and golden as ripe corn – that beard is
named Bellaigue. Ah, the Scudo of the *Revue des deux
mondes* ought to have twisted it seven times round his tongue
before uttering such blasphemies against Wagner . . . But
much will be forgiven him because he did like *Parsifal* . . .
Another critic, that far from handsome little man . . .'

'The one coming towards us, scraping along the walls?'

'If that wall had a reputation, he wouldn't scrape it, he'd
flay it – he's a wriggling, poisonous little snake . . . Oh, how
cantankerous our dear brother is to his brother-critics! When
he isn't writing music, he starts up a perfect hullabaloo of
disgusting rumours.'

'And when he is writing music?'

'He starts up an even more disgusting hullabaloo.'

'*Do* show me some more critics!'

'Ugh! They seem to have astonishingly depraved tastes in
your native bog, my Princess from a far country. No! I won't
show you any more critics because the sole representatives of
French musicography here are limited to the two bipeds I have
just had the honour of . . .'

'What about the others?'

'The others – who number nine hundred and forty-three
and a half (one of them's a legless cripple) – the others never
venture inside a concert-hall . . . it wouldn't be any earthly use
to them if they did. They piously flog their seats to the ticket-
hawkers. They sell their passes and even their "services"! But
let us leave these clod-hoppers and contemplate Madame
Roger-Miclos of the cameo profile, Blowitz of the gorilla face,

Diémer who conceals a piano keyboard, without the black notes, in his mouth, Dutasby the barrister who hasn't missed a single Colonne concert since the day he was weaned.'

'Who's that . . . that lovely creature who positively undulates in her dress?'

'Delila, Messalina, the future Omphale, Austria's share of the spoils.'

'Please?'

'Haven't you read that in old man Hugo? *"L'Angleterre prit Leygues"* . . . I wonder what the hell she got out of it . . . *"et l'Austriche l'Héglon".*'

I knew about *l'aigle* and *l'aiglon* of course, but this pun was beyond me. So I asked: 'And all those other elegant ladies?'

'Nothing, less than nothing. High society and high finance. Gotha and Goldgotha. The pick of the basket and the pick of the pickpockets. They take boxes for the season because it's the thing to do . . . the tiresome thing . . . They're about as musical as skunks and they all jabber loud enough to drown the orchestra – every one of them from the Marquise de Saint-Fiel, who comes here to buck up the artists she gets to perform in her drawing-room with the sight of her, down to the charming Suzanne de Lizery, that well-kept Greuze, "The Broken Pitcher", or the dumb girl who wasn't such a mug as to get broken without being put together with gold rivets. Also known as "the whole duty of man".'

'Why?'

'Because she can't spell.'

Judging I'd been sufficiently bewildered, Maugis went off, at the summons of a friend, to have a well-earned beer in the bar. His throat must have been dry after that eloquence.

I caught sight of Marcel by a pillar in the foyer; he was talking low and fast to a very young man of whom I could see nothing but the nape of a dark neck and very silky hair. I gently pulled my Uncle round the pillar and I recognized the liquid eyes and the white and black face of a certain photograph on the chimneypiece of my 'nephew's' bedroom.

'Uncle, do you know the name of the young man who's talking to Marcel behind the pillar?'

He turned round and swore violently into his moustache.

'Why, it's Charlie Gonzalès of course. He's a bounder, as well as everything else.'

'Everything else?'

'Oh, I mean it's not a friendship I feel exactly overjoyed about for Marcel! That boy could hardly look more flashy!'

The ringing of a bell summoned us back. Marcel rejoined us in our seats. I forgot a great many things to listen to Mademoiselle Pregi poignantly lamenting her desertion, and the orchestra held me enthralled; the orchestra in which Marguerite's heart beat in dull throbs. The Invocation to Nature was encored. This time, Engel imperiously tossed his tempestuous hair and at last roused some response in this audience which had hardly been pretending to listen. My Uncle explained: 'It's because this audience has only heard the *Damnation* seventy-six times!' Marcel, on my left, puckered his mouth discontentedly. When his father is there, he always looks as if he were annoyed with me.

To the accompaniment of an uproar of sound that I found exhausting, Faust rushed towards the Abyss, and we ourselves, shortly after, towards the exit.

It was still daylight outside and the declining sun was dazzling.

'Do you want some tea, children?'

'No, thank you, Father. Do you mind if I leave you now? I've arranged to meet some friends.'

'*Some* friends? That Charlie Gonzalès, I presume.'

'Charlie and others,' Marcel answered curtly.

'Run along. Only, you know,' added my Uncle, in a lower voice, bending down to his son, 'the day I've had enough of all this, I shan't hesitate to tell you . . . I'm going to stand for a repetition of the Lycée Boileau business.'

What business? I was on fire with curiosity to know. But Marcel did not answer. His eyes were black with concentrated fury as he said good-bye and rushed off.

'Are you hungry, my dear?' my Uncle asked. His disillusioned face had aged in the last few moments.

'No, thank you. I'll go home – if you don't mind putting me in a cab.'

78

'I'll even put myself in it too. I'll take you back.'

As a great favour, I begged to go in one with pneumatic tyres that was just passing; I adore that padded, bouncy feeling as you bowl along on them.

We said nothing. The Uncle stared in front of him with a weary, troubled expression.

'I've got things on my mind,' he said after ten minutes, answering a question I had not asked. 'Talk to me, little girl, distract the old gentleman.'

'Uncle, I'd like to ask you how you come to know those people, Maugis and the others?'

'Because I've trailed about all over the place for the last fifteen or twenty years and because it's easy to get to know people in journalism; in Paris, one makes contacts very quickly.'

'I'd also like to ask you – but if it's indiscreet, you can put me off – what you do in the ordinary way, if . . . if, well, you have a profession? I'd so much like to know.'

'Have I a profession? Alas, I certainly have. I'm the man who "does" the foreign politics in the *Diplomatic Review*.'

'In the *Diplomatic Review*! But that's most frightfully boring! I mean' (what a ghastly brick! I felt myself turning scarlet) 'I mean those are awfully serious articles.'

'Don't try and get out of it! Don't gloss it over! You couldn't say anything more flattering: those saving words shall go down to your credit. All my life, I've been regarded by your Aunt Wilhelmine, and by many others, as a contemptible individual who does nothing but amuse himself and amuse his friends. For the last ten years, I've revenged myself by boring my contemporaries. And I bore them in the way they like best – I am well-documented, I am stereotyped, I am pessimistic, and peevish! I am intoning, Claudine, I am rising once more in my own esteem. I have produced twenty-four articles – two dozen – on the scoop of the dispatch from Ems. At present, three times a week for the past six months, I deal with the Russian policy in Manchuria, thus procuring myself necessary cash.'

'It's incredible! I'm nonplussed!'

'And now, why I'm telling you all this, is another affair. I believe that, under the absurd ambition to appear a grown-up person who doesn't need advice from anyone, you're as violent and enthusiastic as any lonely little girl. I never expand, as you've seen, with that unfortunate little Marcel, and I'm overflowing with pent-up paternity. That's what's loosened your uncle's tongue.'

The dear man! I wanted to cry. The music, the nervous strain . . . and something else as well. It was a father like that that I missed and needed. Oh, I don't want to speak ill of mine; it isn't his fault if he's a little peculiar. But this one, I should have adored! With the shyness I always feel when I show what little good I may have in me, I took the risk of saying:

'You know, perhaps *I* might be quite a good safety-valve . . .'

'I thought as much, I thought as much.' (His two great arms closed round my shoulders and he laughed, so as not to seem too emotional.) 'I should like people to do things to upset you so that you could come and tell me about them.'

I stayed leaning against his shoulders; the rubber tyres purred over the uneven cobbles along the quays and the jingling awakened romantic ideas of driving at night in a post-chaise.

'Claudine, what would you have been doing at Montigny at this very moment?'

I started. Montigny couldn't have been further from my thoughts.

'At this very moment? Mademoiselle would have been clapping her hands for us to come in for the evening class. For an hour and a half, up to six o'clock, we used to ruin our eyes in the dusk or, worse still, in the light of the two oil-lamps hung much too high up. Anaïs would have been eating pencil-lead or chalk or fir-wood and Luce would have been nagging me, with her cat's eyes, for some of my extra-hot pepper-mints. The room smelt of the four o'clock sweeping, dust sprinkled with water, ink, and unwashed little girl.'

'Really unwashed? You don't mean to tell me you were the one and only exception to this hydrophobia?'

'Well, practically. Anaïs and Luce always seemed to me fairly clean. But the others – of course I didn't know them so well – but, honestly, well-brushed hair and smooth stockings and white tuckers sometimes don't mean a thing, you know.'

'Lord, as if I didn't know! Unfortunately I can't tell to what extent I *do* know.'

'The other girls . . . anyway, most of them . . . didn't have the same ideas as I did about what's dirty and what's clean. Take Célénie Nauphely, for example.'

'Aha! Let's hear what Célénie Nauphely did!'

'Well, Célénie Nauphely used to stand up – she was a big girl of fourteen – at half past three – half an hour before it was time to go . . . and say out loud, looking very serious and self-important, "Mademoiselle, can I go, please? I've got to go and suck my sister.!'

'Merciful heavens! Suck her sister?'

'Yes. Just imagine, her married sister, who was weaning a child, had too much milk and her breast hurt her. So twice a day Célénie used to suck them to relieve her. She pretended she used to spit the milk out again but, all the same, she must have swallowed some of it in spite of herself. Well, the girls used to fuss over her with admiring envy, this suckling infant. The first time I heard her telling all about it, I couldn't eat my next meal. Doesn't it have any effect on you?'

'Don't press the point I think it most certainly *will* have an effect on me. You certainly open strange vistas on the Fresnois institutions, Claudine!'

'And Héloïse Basseline who found Claire (the girl who made her First Communion with me), with her feet in water one night, and said "I say, have you gone crazy? T'aint Saturday and look at you, washing your feet!" So Claire answered: "But I wash them every night." Whereupon Héloïse Basseline went off, shrugging her shoulders, and saying: "My dear, you're only sixteen and you're as bad as an old maid. They gets sort of funny manias like that!"'

'God in heaven!'

'Oh, I could tell you lots of other things like that. But decency wouldn't permit.'

'Come, come, an old uncle.'

'No, even so, I'd rather not. By the way, talking of Claire, she's getting married.'

'The girl who washes her feet? At seventeen? She's mad.'

I jibbed at this.

'What's mad about it? At seventeen one isn't a child any more! I might very well get married myself.'

'And to whom?'

Caught unawares, I began to laugh.

'Ah, that's another question! Mr Right is in no hurry to appear. At the moment, my suitors aren't exactly falling over each other. My beauty hasn't made enough general sensation yet.'

Uncle Renaud sighed as he leant right back in his seat.

'Alas, you're not ugly enough, you won't go begging long. Some man will fall in love with that lithe figure and the mystery of those elongated eyes. And I shan't have a niece any more and you'll have made a big mistake.'

'So I mustn't get married?'

'Claudine, don't imagine I'm demanding quite such devotion to an uncle as that. But I do at least beg you . . . don't marry just anyone.'

'All right. Choose me a thoroughly safe, reliable husband yourself.'

'You'd better not count on that!'

'Why not? You're so awfully good to me!'

'Because I don't like seeing particularly nice cakes eaten under my very nose. Get out, my dear, we're there.'

What he had just said was better than all the other compliments. I knew I shouldn't forget it.

Mélie opened the door to us, one breast cupped in her hand. In the book-lair, I found Papa in deep conference with Monsieur Maria. This hairy scholar, whose existence I frequently forget, spends an hour here nearly every morning, but I seldom see him.

When Uncle Renaud had gone, Papa solemnly announced to me:

'My child, I have some excellent news for you.'

Heavens, what sinister plot was he hatching now?

'Monsieur Maria is willing to act as my secretary and to assist me in my labours.' Thank goodness it was only that! Much relieved, I held out my hand to Monsieur Maria.

'I'm delighted, Monsieur. I'm sure your collaboration will be an immense help to Papa.'

I'd never said so much to this shy man before and he took refuge behind his forest of hair, beard, and eyelashes without managing to hide his confusion. I suspect this honest youth of secretly having what Maugis would call a 'crush' on me. This doesn't annoy me. *That* one would never dream of treating me disrespectfully!

I've had yet another letter from Claire, positively drivelling with happiness. 'What fun you must be having!' she wrote, so as to give me the idea she was thinking of me. Having fun? I wouldn't exactly describe it as that . . . It isn't that I'm bored, but I'm not happy. Don't get the idea that I'm in love with Marcel. No. He arouses my defiance, my interest, a touch of contemptuous tenderness and, physically, the desire to touch him. *Just* that. All the time I keep wanting to comb his hair, stroke his cheeks, pull his ears, even stick my nails into him now and then, as I used to do to Luce. Also, as I used to do with her too, I want to put one of my eyes close to one of his, lashes to lashes, so as to see the blue stripes in his irises look as if they were dancing. All the same, when one really thinks it over, he is a little like his father on a smaller scale. Yes, *definitely* on a smaller scale.

And still nothing from Luce. It's really very odd, this prolonged silence!

I now possess a tailored coat and skirt, after two fittings at *New Britannia* with Marcel. Those two fittings were enough to make one die of laughter though I kept a perfectly straight face like a real lady. My 'nephew' was admirable. Sitting on a chair a yard away, in one of the little looking-glass lined fitting-rooms, he made Léone the skirt-fitter and Monsieur Rey the cutter spin round like tops, with an off-handedness I admired. 'The dart on the hips a shade further back, don't you agree, Mademoiselle? Not too long, the skirt – just clearing the ground is plenty long enough for the street. Besides, Mademoiselle doesn't know how to walk in very long skirts yet . . .' (A venomous glance from Claudine who said not a word.) 'Yes, the sleeve hangs well. Two little curved pockets on the jacket, to slip her thumbs into when her hands are empty. Claudine, for heaven's sake, keep still for two seconds! Fanchette would fidget less than you do!' The fitter, hypnotized, didn't know what to think. Crouching on all fours on the carpet, she kept glancing up, obviously asked herself: 'He's not her brother because he doesn't say *tu* to her but could he be her gigolo?' And when we went off together after the last trying-on, 'the final fitting', Claudine stiff in her white-collared shirt and wearing a 'boater' that failed to subdue her short hair, Marcel said to me, with a sidelong glance:

'I know what you look like, Claudine, but I'll keep my opinion to myself.'

'Why? You may as well go on now you've started.'

'Certainly not! Respect, family feeling! But that starched collar and that short, curly hair and that straight skirt . . . Oh dear, oh dear! Papa" quite capable of frowning at all that.'

Uneasy at once, I asked:

'You think he wouldn't like it?'

'Oh, he'd get used to it. Papa's no saint under all that air of being a champion of outraged morality.'

'Thank heaven he's *not* a saint. But he's got taste.'

'So have *I* got taste,' said Marcel huffily.

'You . . . you've mainly got *tastes*, rather unusual ones, too.'

Marcel gave a forced laugh as we climbed the dreary steps up to the Rue Jacob. My 'nephew' gladly agreed to come and have something to eat in my room. We settled down with our laps full of Turkish Delight, over-ripe bananas, cold drinks, and salty biscuits. It was hot out-of-doors and cool in my dark bedroom. I risked asking something I'd been keeping back for several days.

'Marcel, what was the business of the Lycée Boileau?'

With his elbow on the arm of the tub-chair and the salt biscuit he was nibbling held between the tips of his slim fingers, Marcel twisted round like a lizard and stared at me. His cheeks were flaming. With his eyebrows drawn together and his mouth open in surprise, what a beautiful little angry god he was! 'Tiny as a clove of garlic,' but so handsome!

'Ah, so you've heard about that! My compliments. You've got sharp ears. I might reply that . . . it's none of your business.'

'You might. But I'm too nice for you to give me such a nasty answer.'

'The business of the Lycée Boileau? A piece of sheer infamy that I shan't forget as long as I live. My father . . . perhaps this'll teach you to know him better, as you're so keen on him. What he did to me over that was something absolutely unforgivable.'

It was incredible how angry and miserable that boy looked! I was absolutely boiling with curiosity.

'*Do* tell me the whole story.'

'Well, you know who I mean by Charlie?'

'I most certainly do!'

'Right. When I first went to the Lycée Boileau as a day-boy, Charlie was due to leave the next year. All those untidy boys with their red wrists and dirty collars simply disgusted me! He was the only one . . . I had the impression that he was like me, and hardly much older! For along time he used to look at me without speaking to me, and then, for no earthly reason, we suddenly became friends. It's impossible to resist the attraction of those eyes. I was obsessed by him without daring to tell him and – I have to believe this –' whispered Marcel, drooping his eyelashes, 'he was obsessed by me, because . . .'

'He told you so?'

'No, he wrote it to me, alas! But wait. I answered, you can imagine how gratefully! And, after that, we used to see each other outside school, at Grandmother's, and other places. And he taught me to know and love hundreds of things I didn't know existed.'

'Hundreds!'

'Oh, don't jump to conclusions and imagine any *Luceries*,' protested Marcel, putting out his hand. 'Exchanges of ideas, of annotated books, or little souvenirs.'

'Go on, schoolgirl!'

'All right, schoolgirl if you like. But most of all, that exquisite correspondence . . . we wrote almost daily . . . until the day . . .'

85

'Ah, *that* was what I was dreading!'

'Yes. Papa stole one of my letters . . .

'*Stole* is going a bit far.'

'Oh, all right, he said he picked it up off the floor. Anyone less evil-minded than he is might perhaps have guessed that all that affectionate way of writing was . . . was purely poetic. But not he! He flew into a really brutish rage – oh! when I think of it, I don't think there's any injury in the world I wouldn't do him – he hit me! And not only that – he went off to make, as he said, "the hell of a row" at the school.'

'Which you were . . . politely asked to leave?'

'Much worse than that. No, it was Charlie who was expelled. They had the insolence! Otherwise Papa would probably have made "the hell of a row" in his filthy news-papers. He's quite capable of it.'

Avidly, I listened, and admired. His red cheeks, his blue eyes, almost black with fury, and that quivering mouth, its corners tense, perhaps, with a desire to cry. I should never see any girls as lovely as Marcel!

'The letter! Your father kept that of course?'

He gave a forced laugh.

'Oh, he wanted to, all right! But I'm cunning too. I got it back from him, with a key that opened his drawer.'

'Oh! Show it me! Do, *do*!'

With an instinctive gesture towards his breast-pocket, he replied:

'Unfortunately I can't, my dear. I haven't go it on me.'

'On the contrary, I'm absolutely certain you have. Marcel, my pretty Marcel, it would be shocking ingratitude for the trust, the beautiful trust your friend Claudine reposes in you!'

I slid insidious hands over him and made my eyes as coaxing as I knew how.

'Little pickpocket! You're not going to take it from me by force? Did one ever see such a girl! I say, let go, Claudine, you'll break one of my nails. Yes, you're going to be shown it. But promise you'll forget it?'

'I swear. By Luce's head!'

He drew out a woman's card-case, Empire green, and

extracted a sheet of very thin paper, carefully folded, and scrawled over in minute handwriting.

I gave myself up to savouring the 'poetry' of Charles Gonzalès.

My Darling,

I am going to look up that story of Auerbach's and I shall translate for you the passages that describe the passionate friendship of the two children. I know German as well as I know French, so this translation won't give me the least difficulty. I almost regret this because it would have been a delight to me to endure some hardships for you, my only loved one.

Oh, yes, my only one! My only loved, my only adored one! And to think your jealousy, always on the alert, is flaring up again! Don't say it isn't, I know how to read between your lines as I know how to read the depths of your eyes and I cannot misunderstand the irritable little sentence in your letter about 'the new friend with the too-black curls whose conversation absorbed me so much at the four o'clock break'.

This so-called new friend – actually I hardly know him – this little boy 'with the too-black curls' (why too?) is a Florentine, Giuseppe Bocci, whom his parents have sent as a boarder to B——, the celebrated philosophy beak, to remove him from the depravity of school friendships; he's certainly got far-seeing parents! This child was telling me about an amusing psychological study one of his compatriots has devoted to the Amicizie del Collegio *which this transalpine Karafft-Ebing apparently defines as a 'mimicry of the passionate instinct' – for these materialists, Italian, German, or French, all manifest the most disgusting, sham-medical imbecility.*

As the pamphlet contains some amusing observations, Giuseppe is going to lend it to me. I asked for it for whom? For you, of course, for you who reward me with this monstrous suspicion. Do you realize how unjust you've been? Then kiss me. Or don't you realize it? In that case, it's I who kiss you.

What a lot of books have been concocted already, all dealing more or less clumsily with this most fascinating and complex question in the world!

To steep myself once more in my faith and my sexual religion, I have re-read Shakespeare's burning sonnets to the Earl of Pembroke and Michelangelo's no less idolatrous ones to Cavalieri. I've also fortified myself by re-reading passages in Montaigne, Tennyson, Wagner, Walt Whitman, and Carpenter.

My slender, my adorable child, my supple, living Tanagra, I kiss your throbbing eyes. You know very well that all that unwholesome past I sacrificed without hesitation for you, all that past with its degrading curiosities that now I loathe, seems to me today like some distant, horrible nightmare. Only your tenderness remains, inspiring me, firing me.

Hell! I've got exactly a quarter of an hour left in which to study 'The Conceptualism of Abelard'. His conceptions must have been of a somewhat peculiar kind, after what he'd had cut off.

Yours body and soul,
    Your Charlie

When I had finished, I did not know what to say. I was slightly alarmed by these goings-on between boys. It didn't astonish me in the least that Marcel's father should have 'flared up' too . . . Oh, I was aware – only too aware – that my 'nephew' was extremely tempting – rather more than tempting, even. But the other one? So Marcel kissed him, kissed this phrasemongering, plagiarizing Charlie, in spite of the little black moustache? Marcel must be anything but ugly when one kissed him. I gave him a covert glance before handing back the letter: he wasn't thinking about me at all; he wasn't even considering asking my opinion. With his chin resting on his hand, he was pursuing some private train of thought. His resemblance to my cousin Uncle, obvious at that moment, suddenly upset me and I gave him back the sheets of paper.

'Marcel, your friend writes that sort of letter more prettily than Luce does.'

'Yes . . . But aren't you shocked at such stupid prudery? Punishing an exquisite person like Charlie!'

'Shocked isn't perhaps quite the word, but I am surprised. After all, though there can only be one Marcel in this world, I imagine schools must include other Charlies.'

'Other Charlies! Look, Claudine, you can't possibly compare him with those dirty schoolboys who . . . I say, give me something to drink and a piece of Delight! Thinking about all this has made me hot.'

He mopped himself with a little blue linen handkerchief. As I hastily offered him a cool drink, he put his card-case down on the wicker table beside him and leant back, feverishly sipping his drink in tiny mouthfuls. He sucked a rose-flavoured piece of Turkish Delight, nibbled a salted biscuit, and lost himself in memories of his Charlie. As for myself, I was so bitten with curiosity that I could have screamed; I asked myself what other letters there might well be in the Empire-green card-case. Now and then (not often, thank heaven) I am seized with these ugly and violent desires to possess something, as fierce as temptations to steal. Certainly, I was perfectly well aware that if Marcel caught me in the act of rummaging among his letters, he would have the right to despise me, and would certainly exploit it, but the thought of this did not make the crimson flush of shame overspread my brow as is customary in all school stories. Sad, but true! With careful negligence, I laid a plate of cakes down on the tempting card-case. If it worked, it worked.

'Claudine,' said Marcel, waking up, 'my grandmother finds you very unsociable.'

'It's true. But I don't know how to talk to her. I can't help it . . . she's practically a stranger to *me* . . .'

'Anyway, all that isn't of the slightest importance . . . Heavens! What an ugly shape Fanchette's getting!'

'Be quiet! My Fanchette is always beautiful. She's very fond of your father.'

'I'm not surprised . . . he's so sympathetic!'

He stood up as he made this amiable remark. He slipped the scrap of linen into his left pocket . . . would he? He'd forgotten about it. If only he'd hurry up and go! For a second,

89

I remembered Anaïs's half-burned love-letters that a similar fit of curiosity had made me take out of the school stove, but I felt not the slightest remorse. Anyway, he'd been sarcastic about his father – he was a horrid little boy!

'Are you going? Already?'

'Yes, I must. And, I assure you, I'm always sorry to go. Because you're the confidante I've always dreamed of – and hardly a bit like a woman!'

Could anything be more charming! I accompanied him as far as the stairs to make sure that the door was duly shut and that he would have to ring the bell if he came up again.

I rushed to the little card-case. It smelt good; Charlie's scent, I presumed.

In one pocket, there was a photograph of Charlie. A half-length postcard-size portrait with bare shoulders and a classical fillet binding his brow and the date '28th December'. I looked up the calendar: '28th December, the Holy Innocents.' Certainly, there were some odd coincidences in the almanack!

There was a bundle of little blue express letters in spiky, pretentious writing and hit-or-miss spelling; meetings arranged or postponed. Two telegrams signed . . . Jules! Well, I never! Here was something that would have made Anaïs gasp till she nearly dislocated her jaw! Along with these letters, there was a woman's photograph! Who was she? An extremely pretty creature, excessively slim, with streamlined hips, wearing a discreetly low-cut dress of sequin-studded black lace. With her fingers on her lips, she was blowing a kiss. Under the photograph, the same signature . . . Jules! I simply had to look closer into this! I sharpened my eyes; I went off and fetched Papa's venerable triple magnifying-glass; I examined the picture minutely. 'Jules's' wrists seemed a trifle thick perhaps, but not as shockingly so as Marie Belhomme's, to quote only one feminine example; those hips could not be masculine, nor could those rounded shoulders, and yet – and yet – the muscles of the neck under the ear made me hesitate again. Yes, it was definitely the neck of a very young man, I could see it now . . . Well, that was that! . . . I continued my rummaging.

On the sort of paper a cook uses and written in a cook's style and with a cook's spelling, was some obscure information.

Take my tip and give the rue Traversière a miss, but you wont run no risk cumming with me to Léons. His place is nice and handy for the Brasserie I was tellig you of and youll see persons there as is worth your while, stable lads from Medrano, eccetera. As to Ernestine and that Weevil, watch out! I don't think Victorine has drawn lotts yet for army service. Rue Lafite, granny will have told you the hotel is saife.

What an extraordinary world! It was this pack of shady characters that Charlie had 'sacrificed' to Marcel! And he dared to make capital out of it! What staggered me most of all was that my 'nephew' did not find it revolting to accept the dregs of an affection that swilled round Weevils, soldiers, grooms 'eccetera'. On the other hand, I understood to perfection that Charlie, sick at last of the too-compliant Juleses – all the same, that incredible photograph! – should have found the novelty adorable. A child who offered him an emotion he had never know before, a child whose scruples it would be delicious to overcome.

He definitely repelled me, this Charlie. My cousin Uncle was perfectly right to get him kicked out of the Lycée Boileau. A dark boy like that probably had hair on his chest!

'Mélie! Quick, run over to Aunt Coeur's! Take a cab – it's to take this little parcel to Marcel with a letter I'm writing to him. You're not to leave it with the porter.'

'A letter, gracious me! Of course I'll take it up my own self! You're a lovely girl. Don't fuss yourself, my pet, it'll get there safe! And no one won't be any the wiser!'

I could safely trust her. Her devotion blazed up at the thought that I was about to kick over the traces. I had no intention of disillusioning her. It gave her so much pleasure.

All the same, it is true that Fanchette is becoming ridiculous to look at! She accepts her 'Parisian' basket on condition that

I leave a piece of my old velveteen dressing-gown in it. She kneads this rage energetically, sharpens her claws on it, keeps it warm in a ball under her, or licks it as she dreams of her future family. Her little breasts are swelling and becoming painful; she is possessed by a constant, insatiable craving to be petted and 'fussied' as they say in Montigny.

Mélie, jubilant, brought me back a note from Marcel, thanking me for the return of the card-case. 'Thank you, dear, I wasn't worried' (*I don't think!*) 'knowing the card-case was in your little hands which I kiss affectionately, discreet Claudine.'

'Discreet Claudine.' That might be sarcastic as well as an appeal to me to keep silence.

Papa is working with Monsieur Maria; that is to say he is wearing the unfortunate young man out by turning out his books from top to bottom. First of all, he had nailed up twelve shelves on the library wall, to the accompaniment of much swearing, twelve shelves designed to take decimo-octavo volumes. A splendid job! Only, when Monsieur Maria, mild, devoted, and dusty, wanted to put the volumes on them, he discovered that Papa had made a mistake of a centimetre in the distance between the shelves so that the books could not stand upright. The result was that all the shelves except one had to be taken down again. You can imagine the stormy cries of 'God's thunderbolts!' and 'Come down, Eternal Father!' Personally, I was convulsed with laughter over this catastrophe. And all that the divinely patient Monsieur Maria said was: 'Oh, it's nothing. We'll just space out the eleven shelves a little more.'

Today I received a lovely great box of chocolate creams, bless him, with a letter from my cousin Uncle.

My charming little friend, your old uncle is sending you this box to make his farewells in his stead. I am sure you won't complain of the substitute. I have to go away on business for eight or ten days. On my return, if you are willing, we will explore some other ill-ventilated haunts for pleasure. Take good care of Marcel who, I'm not joking, gains much from your company. An avuncular kiss on both your paws.

Yes? Well, *I'm* not joking, I'd rather have an uncle and no chocolates. Or, better still, an uncle *and* chocolates. Anyway, these are superb. Luce would sell herself for half the box. Now then, Fanchette, if you want me to murder you, you've only to go on doing that! That wicked creature keeps dipping an only too efficient paw, curved like a spoon, into the open box. Yet all she'll get are half-shells of chocolates, after I've scooped the cream out with the big end of a new pen-nib.

I haven't seen Marcel for two days. A little ashamed of my laziness about going to see Aunt Wilhelmine, I set off, none too eagerly, to visit her. However, I was dressed to my entire satisfaction. I am delighted with my smoothly-fitting tailored skirt and my light blue zephyr blouse that gives my skin a golden tone. Before saying good-bye to me, Papa enunciated solemnly.

'Be sure and tell my sister that I'm up to my eyes in work and that I haven't got a minute to myself so that she doesn't take it into her head to come and bore me under my own roof! And if anyone is impertinent to you in the street *in spite* of your tender years, give them a good clout on the jaw!'

Armed with this sage advice, I went to sleep for forty minutes in the respectable and evil-smelling Panthéon-Courcelles bus and only woke up at the terminus. Place Périere. Bother! I almost invariably do that idiotic thing! I had to walk back all the way to the Avenue Wagram where the unfriendly maid stared disapprovingly at my short hair and informed me that 'Madame had just gone out'. What incredible luck! I didn't waste a second making my escape; I fairly hurtled down the staircase without waiting for the lift.

The green Parc Monceau, with its soft lawns veiled in misty curtains of spray from the sprinkler, attracted me, like something good to eat. There were fewer children there than in the Luxembourg. It was better altogether. But those lawns that are swept like floors! Never mind, the trees enchanted me and the warm dampness I breathed in relaxed me. All the same, the climate of Paris is disgracefully hot. But that sound of leaves, how sweet it was!

I sat down on a bench, but an old gentleman whose hair

and moustache had been tinted with a paint-brush, dislodged me by his insistence on sitting on a fold of my skirt and nudging my elbow. Having treated him as an 'old reptile', I walked away with great dignity to another bench. A tiny little telegraph-boy – what on earth was he doing there? – engaged in hopping from one foot to the other and kicking a flat pebble along, stopped and stared at me and screeched: 'Ooh, aren't you a naughty girl? You jolly well run off and hide in my bed!' Evidently, the Parc Monceau wasn't the desert. Oh, why wasn't I sitting in the shade of the forest of Fredonnes! Collapsing on a chair against a tree I fell into a drowse, lulled by the jets of the sprinkler drumming on the broad leaves of the castor-oil plants.

The heat weighed me down and made me feel imbecile, utterly imbecile. Charming, that lady pattering along, but her legs were too short; anyway, three-quarters of the women in Paris have their behinds on their heels. My Uncle was absurd to go off the moment I was beginning to like him so much. My Uncle . . . He has young eyes, in spite of his incipient crow's feet, and a charming way of leaning towards me when he talks to me. He's travelling on business! Business affairs – or another kind. Mélie, who has a practised eye, answered, when I asked her her impression of him: 'Your Uncle's a fine handsome man, my lamby. A real good all-round worker, for sure.'

He must 'trail around' with women, this man with such a sense of duty. Disgusting!

That little woman just passing . . . Her skirt hung well. She had a walk . . . a walk that I recognized. And that round cheek, fringed in the light with a silvery glisten of fine down . . . I recognized that too. That sketchy little nose, those rather high cheekbones . . . My heart turned over. With one bound, I was behind her, shouting at the top of my voice: 'Luce!'

It was incredible, but it really was she! Her cowardice was proof enough for me. At my shout, she boldly jumped backwards and put her elbow over her eyes. My emotion dissolved into a fit of nervous giggles; I grabbed her by both arms. Her little face with the narrow eyes slanting up to the temples flushed to the ears, then suddenly went pale. At last, she gasped: 'What luck it's you!'

I was still holding her by the arms and there was no end to my amazement. How had I ever recognized her? This little slip of a girl whom I'd always seen in a black serge apron and wearing pointed sabots or heavy lace-up shoes, with no hat except the red woollen hood and her hair in a plait on weekdays and a chignon on Sundays – this Luce was wearing a tailored suit better cut than mine, a pale pink blouse of the finest silk under a short bolero, and a toque of draped crinoline-straw, turned up with a bunch of roses, that she certainly hadn't bought at the 'inexpensive hats' counter. There were one or two false notes one didn't see at first glance: a clumsy corset, too stiff and not curved enough; hair too flattened down and with no style about it; gloves that were too tight. She takes five-and-a-halfs and had, no doubt, squeezed herself into fives.

But what was the explanation of all this splendour? No two ways about it, my little friend had definitely launched herself on the lucrative path of misdemeanour. Yet how fresh and young she looked, with no powder on her face and no red on her lips! Standing face to face, staring at each other without saying a word, we must have looked ridiculous. It was Luce who spoke at last.

'Oh, you've had your hair cut off!'

'Yes. You think I look ugly, don't you?'

'No,' she said tenderly. 'You couldn't look ugly if you tried. You're taller. You look ever so nice. But you don't love me any more, do you? You stopped loving me ages ago.'

She had kept her Montigny accent. I listened to it, enchanted, my ears strained to catch her soft, slightly drawling voice. Her green eyes had subtly changed colour ten times since I had been looking at her.

'That's neither here nor there, you little "wurzit"! Hang it all, what are you doing here and why are you looking so marvellous? Your hat's delicious – tip it a bit further forward. You're not alone, are you? Is your sister here?'

'No, she certainly *isn't* here,' replied Luce, with a malicious smile. 'I've ditched the whole lot of them. It's a long story. I'm dying to tell you all about it. Honestly, it's like something out of a novel.'

Her voice betrayed a fathomless pride; it no longer charmed me.

'But tell away, my little piglet! I've got the whole afternoon to myself.'

'What luck! Claudine, please, would you come back to my place?'

'Yes, but on one condition. I shan't find *anyone* there?'

'No, no one. But come along, come along quick. I live in the Rue de Courcelles, only two steps from here.'

With my head in a whirl, I went along with her watching her sideways as we walked. She wasn't very good at holding up her long skirt and she walked with her head a little forward like someone who doesn't feel their hat is very secure. Oh, how much more touching and individual she used to be in a woollen skirt above her ankles, with her plait half-undone, and her slim feet always out of her sabots. Not that she was uglier! I noticed that her freshness and the mutable colour of her eyes produced considerable effect on the male passers-by. She was aware of it; she made eyes, unconsciously, and lavishly, at all the amorous dogs we met. Heavens, how queer it all was! I was treading in a world of unreality.

'You're looking at my parasol,' said Luce. 'Look see, it's got a crystal handle. It cost fifty francs, old thing!'

'Cost whom?'

'Wait till I tell you everything. I must begin at the beginning or I'll get fair moithered.'

I adored these local expressions. Contrasting with the elegant clothes, the country accent produced a startling effect! I understood certain chortles that occasionally burst without warning from my 'nephew' Marcel.

We passed through the main entrance of a new block of flats, loaded with white sculptures and balconies. An enormous lift, all lined with mirrors, which Luce manipulated with nervous respect, swept us up.

To whose home was she taking me?

On the top storey, she rang the bell – hadn't she got a key then? – and walked quickly past a starchy maid, dressed like an English one, in black with a ridiculous little white muslin apron. It was no bigger than a Negro's costume . . . you know, the costume that consists of a small square of woven grass suspended over the stomach by a string.

Luce hurriedly opened one of the doors in the hall; I followed her into a white passage with a dark green carpet: she opened another door, disappeared through it, shut it behind us, and flung herself into my arms.

'Luce! Do you want a slap?' I said, recovering my former authority with considerable difficulty, for she was holding me tight and burrowing her cool nose in my neck, under the ear. She raised her head and, without loosening her arms, said, with an ineffable expression of happy slavery:

'Oh yes! *Do* bet me a little!'

But I no longer felt inclined – or did not yet feel inclined – to beat her. You don't pound a four-hundred-franc tailored coat and skirt with your fists and it would have been a pity to flatten that pretty bunch of roses with a box on the ears. I'd gladly have clawed her little hands . . . but she'd kept her gloves on.

'Claudine! Oh, you don't love me the least little bit any more!'

'I can't love you like that to order. I've got to know who I'm dealing with! That blouse didn't grow on your back of its own accord, did it? And this flat? "Where am I? Is it magic, is it an enchanted dream?" as that beanpole Anaïs used to sing in that acid voice that put one's teeth on edge.'

'This is my bedroom,' answered Luce, in an unctuous voice. She stood back a little so as to let me admire it.

Too sumptuous, but not too absurd, her bedroom. It was well upholstered for instance! There was white enamel – alas! – but there were chairs and wall-panels covered in almond-green velvet with a shell design – a copy of Utrecht, I think – that flattered one's eyes and enhanced one's complexion. The bed – oh! what a bed! I couldn't resist measuring its width with my two outstretched arms: more than a metre and a half. Madame, more than a metre and a half, they say, is a bed for at least three people! Beautiful curtains of almond-green damask at the two windows, a triple-doored wardrobe with a long glass, a little chandelier on the ceiling (it looked idiotic, that little chandelier), and a big white and yellow striped armchair by the fireplace. And goodness knows what else!

'Luce, are these the fruits of dishonour? *You* know . . . "the deceptive fruits that leave a taste of ashes in the mouth", if one can believe our old *Moral Tales*.'

'You haven't seen the most splendid of all,' Luce went on without answering. 'Look!'

She opened one of the doors adorned with little carved garlands. 'This is the bathroom and dressing-room.'

'Thanks. I might so easily have thought it was Mademoiselle Sergent's private oratory.'

Paved with tiles, walled with tiles, the bathroom glittered, like Venice, with a thousand lights (and more). Sakes alive, was it possible? A bath for a young elephant and two tip-up basins as deep as the pond of Barres. On the dressing-table, blonde tortoiseshell that must have cost fantastic sums. Luce rushed to a curious little stool, lifted up the padded top studded with gilt buttons that covered it, like a box-lid, and said ingenuously, displaying the oblong pan, 'It's solid silver.'

'Ugh! The edges must be awfully cold to sit on. Is your coat-of-arms engraved on the bottom? But tell me everything or I'll buzz off.'

'And it's all lit by electricity. *I'm* always frightened of accidents, sparks, something or other that kills you (my sister used to bore us so much with all that stuff at Montigny in physics lessons!). So *when as* I'm all alone at night, I light a little oil lamp. Have you seen my chemises? I've got six silk ones, and the rest Empire with pink ribbons and knickers to match . . .'

'Empire knickers? I didn't think there was a frenzied demand for them in these days . . .'

'Oh yes, because the sewing-maid told me that they were Empire, so there! And then . . .' Her face sparkled. She fluttered from one cupboard to another, getting tangled up in her long skirt. Suddenly she pulled up her rustling petticoats with both hands and whispered to me ecstatically: 'Claudine, I've got *silk stockings*!' She had, indeed, silk stockings. They were silk, as I could verify, right up to the thighs. I remembered her legs very well, the little marvels.

'Feel how soft it is!'

'I take your word for it, I take your word for it. But I swear I'll go away if you keep rambling on like this without saying anything!'

'Then let's make ourselves comfortable. Here, in the armchair, plumpy you down. Just a twit, while I pull down the blind, 'cos of the sun.'

They were priceless, her lapses into her native speech. In her pink blouse and her impeccable skirt, the effect was pure comic-opera.

'Shall we have a drink? I always keep two bottles of tonic wine in my bathroom. *He* says that'll stop me from getting anaemic.'

'*He*! There's a *He*! What luck, now I shall know all! The portrait of the seducer . . . go and fetch it this minute.'

Luce went out and returned with a frame in her hand.

'There, that's him,' she said without enthusiasm.

It was hideous, this cabinet photo of a fat, almost bald, man of about sixty, perhaps more. He had a bestial look, with jowls like a Great Dane and big calf's eyes! Horrified, I stared at my little friend who was silently contemplating the carpet and fidgeting with one foot.

'Old thing, you've got to tell me all. It's even more interesting than I thought.'

Sitting at my feet on a cushion, in the gilded dusk of the lowered blinds, she clasped her hands on my knees. The change in the way she did her hair upset me very much; besides she should never have had it waved. I, in turn, took off my boater and ruffled up my curls to give them some air. Luce smiled at me.

'You look exactly like a boy, Claudine, with your short hair, a jolly nice-looking boy, too! Yet no, when one really looks at you, you've definitely got a girl's face. Yes, a pretty girl's!'

'That'll do. Get on with the story, from the very first scrap right up to today. And do buck up a bit, otherwise Papa will think I've got lost or run over.'

'Yes. Well, when you decided to write to me after your

illness, *they* were already being as beastly as possible to me. And this and that, and I was a goose and I was a caricature of my sister, and all the time they kept calling me names.'

'Are they still getting on well together, your sister and the Headmistress?'

'Goodness me, worse than ever. My sister doesn't even sweep her room any more. Mademoiselle has taken on a little servant girl. And on the least excuse, Aimée pretends she's ill and doesn't come downstairs and it's Mademoiselle who takes her place for nearly all the oral lessons. Better than that: one evening, in the garden, I heard Mademoiselle making a terrible scene with Aimée about a new assistant master. She lost all control of herself: "One of these days I'll kill you," she said to Aimée. And my sister burst out laughing and said, looking at her sideways: "You wouldn't dare, you'd be too sorry afterwards." And then Mademoiselle began to "blub" and implored her not to torture her any more and Aimée flung her arms round her neck and they went indoors together. But it wasn't all *that* stuff, I was used to that. Only, I tell you, my sister treated me like a dog and so did Mademoiselle. When I started to ask for some shoes and stockings, my sister sent me packing. "If the feet of your stockings are in holes, mend them" – that's what she said to me. "Besides, the legs are good still and as long as the holes can't be seen, it's as if they didn't exist." It was the same thing with dresses; she had the cheek, the filthy beast, to foist off an old blouse on me that had all gone under the arms. I cried all day because my clothes were in such an awful state; I'd rather have been beaten! Once I wrote home. They never have a penny, as well you know. Mum wrote back: "Fix things up with your sister, you cost us enough money as it is. Our pig has died of disease and I had fifteen francs to pay the chemist last month for your little sister Julie. You know that at home it's poverty and trouble of every kind, so, if you're hungry, eat your fist."'

'Go on.'

'One day, when I'd tried to frighten my sister, she ended up by laughing in my face and bawling at me: "If you don't like it here, why don't you go back home then? You could look after the geese. It would be good riddance for us." That day,

100

I couldn't eat my dinner or get to sleep. The next morning, after class, as I was going up to the refectory, I found Aimée's bedroom door ajar. Her purse was lying on the mantlepiece, by the clock (for she's got a clock, my dear, the dirty pig!). Seeing it there suddenly made my blood run cold. I pounced on the purse but she'd have been sure to search me and I didn't know where to hide it. I'd still got my hat on, I put on my jacket and I went down to the lavatories and threw my apron down one. I went out again without meeting anyone (everyone was in the refectory by then), and I ran off on foot to catch the 11.39 train to Paris. It was just on the point of starting. I was half-dead from running.'

Luce paused for breath and to enjoy the effect of her story. I admit I was stunned. Never would I have believed that chit capable of such impulsive action.

'What next? Hurry up, child, what next? How much was there in the purse?'

''Twenty-three francs. So, when I got to Paris, I had nine francs left. I'd taken third-class tickets, of course. But wait. Everyone knew me at the station and old Racalin asked me: "Where are you running off to like that, my little dear?" I told him: "My mother's ill . . . they sent us a telegram . . . I'm hurrying off to Sementran, my sister can't get away." And he said, 'That's very worrying for you.'"

'But, once you'd reached Paris, what did you do?'

'I went out of the station and I walked. I asked where the Madeleine was.'

'Why?'

'You'll see. Because my uncle – that's him in the photo, lives in the Rue Tronchet, near the Madeleine.'

'Your mother's brother?'

'No, her brother-in-law. He married a rich woman who's dead now. He's made simply piles of money himself too, and, of course, he didn't so much as want to hear us starving relations mentioned any more. You'd expect that. I knew his address because Mum, who'd an eye on the money, forced us to write to him, all five of us, on New Year's Day, on flowered paper. So I only went to his place to know where to sleep.'

' "Where to sleep!" Luce, my homage! You're a hundred times wickeder than your sister, and than me too.'

'Oh! Wicked? That's not the right word. I just fell into it. I was dying of hunger. I had on Aimée's little old blouse and my school hat. And I found a flat *even* more grand than this one and a manservant who asked me, all sharp like: "What do you want?" I felt ashamed, I wanted to cry. I said: "I want to see my uncle." Do you know what he said to me, that beast? "Monsieur has given me orders not to admit any of his relations!" Wasn't it enough to strike you dead? I turned round to go away, but I found myself face to face with a fat gentleman who was just coming in. So from then on, there was no going back! "What's your name?" – "Luce." "Did you mother send you?" – "Oh, no. I came all on my own. My sister was making me so unhappy that I've run away from school." – "From school? How old are you then?" he asked, and he took me by the arm and made me come into the dining-room. "I'll be seventeen in four months' time." – "Seventeen? You don't look it, far from it. What a strange story! Sit down, my child, and tell me all about it." So then, you see, naturally I brought it all out, how miserable I'd been, and Mademoiselle, and Aimée, and the holey stockings, well, the whole lot. He listened and he kept looking at me with his big blue eyes and he kept pulling his chair up closer. Towards the end, I was so tired that I started to cry! And here was a man who took me on his knees and kissed me and said nice things to me. "Poor little thing! It's a shame to torment such a nice little girl. Your sister takes after her mother; mark my words, she's a pest. Hasn't she got lovely hair! With her pigtail, you'd say she was fourteen." And little by little there he was stroking my shoulders and hugging my waist and my hips and kissing me all the time and puffing like a grampus. It disgusted me a bit, but I didn't want to annoy him, you understand.'

'I understand perfectly. What happened next?'

'What happened next . . . oh, I couldn't tell you *everything*.

'Don't be a little hypocrite! You weren't such a prude at school!'

'It's not the same thing. *Before*, he made me dine with him

– I was dying of hunger. Such good things, Claudine! "Goodies" of all kinds – and champagne. After dinner, I'd no idea what I was saying. *He* was as red as a cock, but he didn't get flustered. He came out fair and square with his proposition: "My little Luce, I'll promise to put you up for a week, to inform your mother – in a way that won't start her yapping – and, later on, to arrange a nice little future for you. But on one condition; you'll do whatever I want you to do. You look to me as if you didn't despise the good things of life and liked your comforts – that goes for me too. If you're absolutely untouched, so much the better for you, because then I'll be nice to you. If you've already trailed around with boys, nothing doing! I've got my ideas and I stick to them."'

'And then?'

'And then he took me into his bedroom, a lovely red bedroom.'

'And then?' I said avidly.

'And then . . . oh, I can't remember. Honest I can't!'

'Do you want a slap to make you talk?'

'Well,' said Luce, shaking her head, 'actually it's not so funny, you know.'

'Ah? Does it really hurt very much?'

'It certainly does! I "gave tongue" with all my might and besides his face right up against mine made me hot and his hairy legs scratched me. And he puffed and he panted! As I was "giving tongue" too much, he said, in a choky voice, "If you don't scream, I'll give you a gold watch tomorrow." I tried not to make another sound. Afterwards, I was so all to bits that I cried out loud. *He* kept kissing my hands and saying: "Swear to me that no one else shall ever have you. I'm too lucky for words, too lucky for words!" But *I* wasn't awfully happy.'

'Difficult, aren't you?'

'And then, in spite of myself, all the time I kept thinking about the rape at Ossaire – you remember *that* – the bookseller in Ossaire who raped one of his shopgirls. When the case was on we used to read the *Fresnois Monitor* in secret and we used to learn some sentences by heart. All the same, they did come up at quite the wrong moment, those memories.'

103

'Stop being literary and get on with the rest of the story.'

'The rest of the story? Oh dear! . . . Well, the next morning, I just couldn't get over seeing this fat man in my bed. He's so ugly when he's asleep! But he's never been really nasty and sometimes we even have good moments . . .' Luce's lowered eyelids hid eyes that were knowing and hypocritical. I waned to question her, yet, at the same time, I was embarrassed. Surprised at my silence, she looked at me.

'Come on, Luce, get on with it!'

'All right. Well, at first my family tried to find me. But my uncle wrote to them straight away. "My little darling, I simply warned your mother to leave us in peace and not poke her nose in if she wanted to see the colour of my money after I'm dead. As for you, you can do whatever you like. You've twenty-five louis a month, your food, and your clothes. Send them some brass or don't send it them, I don't give a damn either way! But *I* won't send them a farthing!"'

'So you did send some money home?'

Luce's face became diabolical.

'What *me*? You don't know me! Oh no thanks, I'm too fed up with all they've done to me! Let them starve, d'you hear? . . . starve! I'd see them all starve to death without drinking one single drop less myself! Oh, they haven't denied themselves the pleasure of asking me for money . . . oh ever so nicely, with ever such good manners. D'you know what I answered? I took a sheet of white paper – a big one and I wrote on it: S——t! Just that!'

She had said the word, a word of four letters.

She stood up and danced about, her pretty pink face positively lit up with ferocity. I couldn't get over it.

Could this really be that timid girl I had known at school, that poor younger sister who was beaten by Aimée, the favourite, that little Luce of the soft, coaxing ways who was always wanting to kiss me in the wood-shed? I wondered whether to leave then and there. This little girl and her uncle, it was all too modern for me. According to her, she'd actually have let them die of starvation!

'Honestly, Luce, you'd let them . . .'

'Oh! yes, Claudine darling. What's more,' she added, with

a forced laugh, 'if you only knew, I'm working on my uncle to cut them right out of his will! Isn't that screamingly funny?'

Obviously, it was screamingly funny.

'So, you're utterly and completely happy?'

She broke off her waltz and pulled a face.

'Utterly and completely? There are snags. I still have to go carefully with my uncle! He's got a way of saying: "If you don't want to, it's all up between us!" that forces me to do as I'm told.'

'If you don't want to what?'

'Nothing -lots of things,' she answered, with a sweeping gesture. "But he gives me money, too, that I hide under a pile of chemises and, most of all, oh! most of all, sweets and pastries and little birds to eat. And even better than that, champagne at dinner.'

'Every night? Your skin will get blotchy, my dear!'

'Do you think so? Just take a good look at me . . .'

It was true that no flower could be fresher. Luce's skin is genuine fast-dyed material, guaranteed not to spot in rain – or even in mud.

'Tell me, dear Madame. Do you receive company? Do you give dinner-parties?'

Her face darkened.

'Not possible, with that jealous old thing! He doesn't want to let me see anyone at all. But' (she lowered her voice and spoke with a smile that told much), 'one can manage things all the same. I've seen my little friend, Caïn Brunat – you know, the one you used to call my "flirt". He's at the Beaux-Arts, he ought to become a great painter, and he's doing my portrait. If you only knew . . .' she said, with her birdlike volubility. 'He's old, my uncle, but he has impossible ideas. Sometimes he makes me get down on all-fours and run about the room like that. And he runs after me on all-fours too, looking like a comic caricature with his great fat stomach. Then he jumps on me, bellowing: "I'm a wild beast! . . . look out for yourself! I'm a bull!"'

'How old is he?'

'Fifty-nine, so *he* says. A bit more, I think.'

My head was aching. I was stiff all over. This Luce was too

disgusting. You should have seen her describing these horrors! Perched on one foot, with her fragile hands spread wide, a pink ribbon belt buckled round her tiny waist and her soft hair combed back smoothly from her transparent temples, the pretty little boarding-school Miss.

'Luce, while you're off the chain, *do* give me some news of Montigny. Please! No one ever talks to me about it any more. How's that gawk Anaïs?'

'Much as usual; nothing special. She's "going with" one of the Third Years.'

'Not too squeamish a Third Year, I bet! And Marie Belhomme and her midwife's hands? Remember, Luce, when she owned up to us that in summer she didn't wear any drawers so as to fell her thighs "stroke each other" when she walked?'

'Yes, I remember *that*. She's serving in a shop. No luck, poor girl!'

'Everyone can't have your luck, you little prostitute!'

'I don't like people to call me that,' Luce protested, shocked.

'All right then, shy virgin, tell me about Dutertre.'

'Oh, that poor doctor, he flirted with me every such a lot towards the end . . .'

'Well? Why not?'

'Because my sister and Mademoiselle had sent him packing good and proper and my sister said to me: 'If *that* happens to you, I'll scratch your two eyes out!" He's having a lot of worries over his politics.'

'So much the better! What worries?'

'Hark you now to this story. At a meeting of the Town Council, Dutertre got caught out over the station at Moustier. If he didn't want to go and have it put two kilometres away from the village because that would have been more convenient for Monsieur Corne – you know, the owner of that lovely château on the edge of a road – who'd given him goodness knows how much money!'

'Just like his impudence!'

'So, in the Council, Dutertre tried to carry that through as something quite reasonable and the others didn't kick up any fuss, when suddenly Dr Fruitier, a thin, dried-up old man, a bit loony, got up and treated Dutertre like the lowest of the low. Dutertre gave him a pretty rough answer, a bit too rough, and Fruitier slapped him right in the face in front of the whole Council!'

'Ah, ah! I can see him from here, old Fruitier! His little white hand – it's all bones – must have made a splendid *clack*!'

'Yes, and Dutertre, absolutely beside himself, kept rubbing his cheek and gesticulating and yelling: "I shall send my seconds to challenge you!" But old Fruitier calmly replied: "One doesn't fight a duel with a Dutertre, don't force me to print the reason why in all the local papers!" There was a terrific hullabaloo about it in our part of the world, I can tell you.'

'I bet there was. Did Mademoiselle make herself ill over it?'

'She'd have died of rage if my sister hadn't consoled her, but the things she said about it! As she wasn't a native of Montigny, there was no stopping her. "Filthy hole full of brigands and thieves!" And so on and so forth . . .'

'And Dutertre? Is he a figure of public scorn?'

'Him! Two days afterwards, no one gave it another thought: he hasn't lost *that* of his influence. And the proof is, that at one of the last Council meetings, they got round to talking about the School and saying it was run in a very peculiar way. You realize, all Mademoiselle's goings-on with Aimée are known all over the countryside now: no doubt some of the big girls must have gossiped about it . . . so much so that one of the Councillors demanded that Mademoiselle should be dismissed. Whereupon my Dutertre stood up and announced: "If the Headmistress is called to account, I shall make it my personal business." He didn't say anything more but they understood and they started talking about other things because, you know, they're nearly all under some obligation to him.'

'Yes, and, besides, he's got them by all sorts of dirty things he knows about them.'

'Still it didn't stop his enemies fairly rushing at it or the parish priest talking about it in his sermon the very next Sunday.'

'Old Father Millet? Right out in the pulpit? But Montigny must have been put to fire and sword!'

'Yes, indeed. The priest, he shouted: "Shame on the scandalous object-lessons lavished on youth in your Godless schools!" Everyone realized he was talking about my sister and the Headmistress and, of course, they thoroughly enjoyed it!'

'More, Luce, tell me more. You rejoice my heart.'

'Goodness, I can't think of any more. Liline had twins last month. They gave a big official reception for Hémier's son who came home on leave from Tonkin where he's landed an awfully good job. Adèle Tricotot's now got a fourth husband. Gabrielle Sandré, who still looks like a little girl with those babyish teeth of hers, is getting married in Paris. Lénie Mercant is an assistant-mistress in Paris (you know who I mean, that tall shy girl – we used to amuse ourselves by making her blush because she had such a thin skin). I tell you, *all* of them are coming to Paris; it's the rage, it's a positive mania.'

'It's not a mania that afflicts me,' I said, with a sigh. 'Personally, I long to be back *there*. Not so much as when I first arrived, though, because I'm beginning to get attached to . . .'

I bit my lips, worried at having said too much. But Luce is not observant and the flow of her conversation went on, in full spate.

'Well, if you long to be back, you're not a bit like *me*. Sometimes, in that huge bed over there, I dream I'm still in Montigny and that my sister's torturing me with her decimal fractions and the mountain-system of Spain and quad-rigeminal peduncles. I wake up in a sweat and I'm always tremendously happy to find I'm here!'

'Beside your kind uncle, who snores.'

'Yes, he does snore. However did you know?'

'Oh, Luce, how disarming you can be! But the School, tell me more about the School. Do you remember the jokes we used to play on poor Marie Belhomme? And that wicked devil, Anaïs?'

'Anaïs, she's at Training College – I've told you that

already. She and her "Third Year", who's called Charretier, are almost like my sister and Mademoiselle. You know, at Training College, the dormitories have two rows of open cubicles, separated by an aisle for the mistress in charge to walk up and down and keep her eye on everyone. At night, they draw a red cotton curtain in front of those cubicles. Well, Anaïs has found a way of going into Charetier's almost every night and she hasn't got caught yet. But it'll end up in disaster. At least, I hope so.'

'How do you know all this?'

'From a boarder who lives near us in Sementran and who went there the same term as Anaïs. Apparently that Anaïs looks frightfully ill – an absolute skelton! She can't find uniform collars small enough to fit her neck. Imagine, Claudine darling, they get up at five there! And I laze in my bye-bye till ten or eleven and I have my morning chocolate there. You know,' she added, looking exactly like a sensible, practical little housewife, 'all that helps one to overlook a lot of things.'

But, in my inward mind, I was still far away in Montigny. Luce had squatted down at my feet like a little hen.

'Luce, what have we got for composition for next time?'

'For next time,' said Luce, bursting into laughter . . . 'we've got: *Write a letter to a girl of your own age to encourage her in her vocation to be a teacher.*'

'No, Luce, that's not it, we've got: *Look below yourself and not above yourself; such is the way to be happy.*'

'Sucks, no, it isn't! It's: *What do you think of ingratitude? Support your opinion by an anecdote invented by yourself.*'

'Is you map finished?'

'No, old thing. Didn't have time to "ink it in". I shall get an awful wigging. Just imagine . . . my mountains aren't hatched and my Adriatic coast isn't finished.'

I hummed: '*Come down to the blue Adriatic . . .*'

'*And bring all your fish-nets on board,*' sang Luce, in her small, liquid voice.

Then both of us sang in parts: '*Come down, bring your fish-nets on board!*'

And we launched into it:

109

'Haste down to the sea! Ye fishers, the tide,
Foams round the rocks as it races:
The trusty boat moored too long to the side,
Rocks in the wavelet's embraces.
To the beach, all ye maids of the village.
The harvest is ripe for the tillage.
Come forth from each cellar and attic,
To linger ye cannot afford,
Come down to the blue Adriatic
And bring all your fish-nets on board.
Come down, bring your fish-nets on board.'

'Do you remember, Luce, that was where Marie Belhomme *always* went down two notes, goodness knows why? She started shaking with apprehension ten bars before, but she invariably got it wrong. Chorus, now!

"Tis a cool and calm night
For the fishers' delight;
Row fast o'er the wave,
Ye fishermen brave!

'And now, Luce, the grand arrival of the catch!

'Here are sardines,
Of our waters the queens,
Here cuttlefish writhe,
Their tentacles lithe
And fish great and small
Heap the glittering haul
Let us sing jubilee
To the generous sea
Who has granted our wish ⎫ *twice*
With such harvest of fish.' ⎭

Carried away with enthusiasm and beating time, we sang this preposterous ballad through to the very end and we burst into roars of laughter like the two children we still were. Nevertheless, I felt a little saddened by these old memories,

110

whereas Luce hopped about ecstatically, giving little squeaks of joy, and admiring herself in 'her' triple-mirrored wardrobe.

'Luce, don't you ever regret the School?'

'The School? Every time I remember it at meals, I ask for more champagne and I eat enough petits-fours to make me sick, to make up for lost time and for all I've had to put up with. Lord, I wish I'd left school for good and all. But I *haven't*, even now!' She pointed gloomily towards a folding-screen. I followed the direction of her finger and saw, half-hidden by the silk and lacquer screen, a little wooden desk with a seat attached to it, just like our school-desks at Montigny. It was ink-stained and littered with grammar and arithmetic books. I rushed to it and opened some exercise books filled with Luce's tidy, childish writing.

'Your old exercise books, Luce! Whatever for?'

'No, not my old exercise books, unfortunately – my new ones! And you'll find my big black apron in the hanging-cupboard in the bathroom.'

'What's the idea?'

'Oh, goodness, it's one of my uncle's fancies, the worst one of all! You'll never believe it. Claudine darling,' groaned Luce, raising two plaintive arms, 'he often makes me do my hair in a plait again and put on a big pinafore and sit down at that desk . . . and then he dictates a problem to me, or the outline of an essay . . .'

'I don't believe you!'

'Oh, but he *does*. And it's not a joke: I have to do sums and write essays. The first time, when I said I wouldn't, he flew into a real temper. "You deserve to be whipped, you're going to be whipped," he kept saying. And his eyes were all shining and his voice was so queer. I was frightened, so I got down to work.'

'So this man's interested in your progress as a scholar, is he?'

'It amuses him, it . . . it gets him going. It makes me think of Dutertre who used to read our French essays and keep putting his fingers down our necks at the same time. But Dutertre was much handsomer than my uncle. *Ever* so much,' sighed poor Luce, doomed to be an eternal schoolgirl.

111

I couldn't get over it! That sham-little girl in a black apron, that old schoolmaster questioning her about decimal fractions.

'Believe it or not, Claudine,' Luce went on, looking gloomier than ever, 'he went for me yesterday, the *beast*, just like my sister at Montigny because I went wrong over some dates in English History. I rebelled, I screamed at him: "English History, that's Higher Certificate, I've had enough!" My uncle didn't raise his eyebrows, he just closed his book and said: "If the pupil Luce wants her piece of jewellery, she must recite the Gunpowder Plot to me without one mistake."'

'And *did* you recite it without one mistake?'

'Lord love us, yes – here's the buckle. It was well worth it – look, see the topazes – and the snake's eyes be little diamonds.'

'But come, come Luce, this is really all most edifying. You'll be able to sit for your "Higher" at the next exam session.'

'Just you wait,' Luce said furiously, shaking her little fist menacingly. 'My family's going to pay for all this. Besides, I got my revenge. After that, I cut down my uncle's rations. Last month, I was "indisposed" for a fortnight. So there!'

'He must have looked decidedly glum!'

'Glum? The things you say!' Luce twittered in delight, leaning back in her armchair and showing all her short little white teeth.

At school she used to laugh just like that when Anaïs had said something extra smutty or spiteful. But personally, I felt shocked. That coarse, fat man she was joking about was too close to us amidst all this tart's luxury. Suddenly, I noticed a charming little crease at the base of her neck that had not been there before.

'Luce, you're putting on flesh!'

'D'you think so? I think I am, too. My skin wasn't exactly black even at Montigny,' she said coquettishly, coming close to me, 'but now it's even whiter. If only I'd got real breasts! But my uncle likes me better flat. All the same, they're a little rounder than they were at our competitions in the hollow lanes, remember, Claudine? . . . Would you like to see?'

She came closer still, her face sparkling and provocative

112

and, with one hand, deftly undid her pink blouse. The skin above the incipient breasts was so find and pearly that it looked bluish against the China rose silk. There were pink ribbons threaded through the lace of the chemise (Empire, don't forget!). And her eyes, those green eyes with black lashes, had become strangely languid.

'Oh, Claudine!'

'What is it?'

'Nothing. I'm so pleased to have found you again! You're even prettier than you were at school, even though you're crueller than ever to your Luce.'

Her soft, coaxing arms turned around my neck. Heavens, how my head ached and throbbed!

'Whatever scent do you use?'

'Chypre. I smell nice, don't I? Oh, do kiss me. You've only kissed me once. You asked me, didn't I regret anything about the School? I do, Claudine, I regret the little shed where we used to break up the firewood at half past seven in the morning and where I used to kiss you, and you used to beat me. You used to thrash me good and hard, you cruel girl! But, all the same, tell me truly, don't you think I'm prettier *now*? I have a bath every morning, I wash myself as much as your Fanchette. Do stay a little longer! Do stay! I'll do absolutely anything you like. Now, put your ear close, let me whisper. I know such lots of things now.'

'*No!*'

She was still rubbing up against me and talking to me when I took her by the shoulders and gave her a brutal push that she tottered back against the handsome three-doored wardrobe and banged her head on it. She rubbed her skull and looked at me, to know whether to cry or not. So I went up to her and gave her a hearty slap. She turned crimson and burst into tears.

'Oh, how *could* you? Whatever have I done?'

'Look here, do you imagine I pick up old men's leavings?' I put on my boater with a shaking hand (I pricked my head hard with the hatpin); I threw my jacket over my arm and I made for the door. Before Luce realized what was happening, I was in the hall and groping to find the front door. Luce flung herself on me, distraught.

113

'Claudine, you're mad!'

'Not in the least, my dear. I'm too old-fashioned for you, that's all. It wouldn't work at all, the two of us. My kindest regards to your uncle.'

And I hurried downstairs as fast as I possible could, so as not to see, Luce, in tears, with her blouse open over her white breast, sobbing out loud and leaning over the banisters, imploring me to come back.

'Comey back, Claudine darling, comey back!'

I found myself in the street with a splitting headache and the dazed feeling you wake up with after some particularly idiotic dream. It was nearly six o'clock. The eternally dusty air of this filthy Paris seemed to me, this evening, soft and clear. What on earth *was* all this story? I wished someone would pull me by the sleeve and wake me up. I wished a Luce in pointed sabots, with her rebellious hair straying in wisps out of the red woollen hood, would say to me, laughing like a child: 'Aren't you a silly, Claudine, to dream such ridiculous things?'

But it was no use, I didn't wake up. And it was the other Luce I kept seeing, weeping and dishevelled and calling to me in her tear-drenched country accent, so much more pretty and so much less touching than the schoolgirl Luce.

But, in spite of everything, what on earth had come over me when that little thing had implored me, with her slim arms twined about my neck? Had I become extraordinarily prudish in the course of a few months? Without mincing words, extraordinarily virtuous? It was not the first time that incorrigible Luce had tempted me nor the first time I had hit her. But a whole flood of feeling had surged up in me. Jealousy, perhaps. A smothered indignation at the thought that this Luce who used to adore me, who still did adore me in her own way, had flung herself into the lap of an old gentleman (no, really, those eyes like a badly-boiled calf's head!). And disgust. Disgust, yes, definitely! There I was, making myself completely sophisticated and disillusioned and shouting from the roof-tops 'Ha, ha! you can't teach *me* anything. Ha, ha! I read *everything*! And *I* understand everything even though I *am* only seventeen!' Precisely. And when it comes to a gentleman pinching my behind in the street or a little friend *living* what I'm in the habit of reading about, I'm knocked sideways. I lay about me with my umbrella or else I flee from vice with a noble gesture. In your heart of hearts, Claudine, you're nothing but a common everyday decent girl. How Marcel would despise me if he knew that!

The Panthéon-Courcelles bus came placidly zigzagging alongside me. Hope! I leapt on it without deigning to wait for it to stop. A successful jump on to the step of a bus going at full trot consoles me for many things. Provided Papa hadn't decided, this one day of all days, to make one of his rare incursions into real life! He might have thought I'd been out rather a long time and it would have upset me to have had to lie to him and tell him I'd spent the afternoon with Aunt Coeur.

My fears were groundless: Papa was up in the clouds as usual. When I went in, he was surrounded by manuscripts, and he merely darted a wild look at me over his forest of beard. Monsieur Maria, almost as quiet as a mouse, was writing at a little table. At the sight of me he furtively pulled out his watch. *He* was the one who had worried over my absence!

'Aha!' cried Papa, in his richest tones. 'You've more than done your duty by the family! You went off at least an hour ago.'

Monsieur Maria gave a distressed glance at Papa. *He* knew that I had gone out at two o'clock and that it was now thirty-five minutes past six.

'Monsieur Maria, you've got eyes like a hare! No, don't take that badly! Hares have very beautiful eyes, black and liquid. Papa, I didn't see Aunt Coeur because she'd gone out. But I've seen something much better, I've re-discovered a little friend from Montigny here. Luce, you remember Luce, don't you? She's living in the Rue de Courcelles.'

'Luce, ah, I've got it! She's the one who's getting married, who made her First Communion with you.'

'More or less right. We talked for ages, as you can imagine.'

'And you'll be going to see her often?'

'No, because I can't stand the furniture in her flat.'

'What's the husband like? Poisonous, eh?'
'I don't know. I only saw his photograph.'

For the last two days, I haven't set foot out-of-doors. I stay in my room or in the book-lair, behind the half-closed shutters that still let in too much heat and too much light. This summer, that has turned threatening, frightens me, I don't know where to hide myself. Suppose I were to fall ill again! I listen to the thunderstorms and, after the showers, I breathe in the damp air, charged with electricity. However boldly I lie to myself, that afternoon with Luce has shaken me more than I like to admit. Mélie, who has given up trying to understand me, aggravates my trouble by talking to me about Montigny; she has had recent and detailed news from there.

'The little girl at Koenet has just had a baby.'

'So? How old is she?'

'Thirteen and a half. A fine boy, it seems. The walnut tree at the top of the garden is going to have lots of nuts.'

'Shut up, Mélie, I shan't be there to eat them.'

'What fine nuts, eh my lamb? Riddle-me-ree, riddle-me-reeks. Two pairs of buttocks in one pair of breeks.'

'Tell me some more news.'

'The big *cuisse-de-nymphe* rose is already eaten up with caterpillars (it's the tenant's manservant as wrote to me) and they're amusing themselves killing them all. He must have a screw loose!'

'Well, what do you expect them to do with them? Make them into jam?'

'Don't you go purtending as you don't know! You takes a caterpillar in your hand, you takes him over to another village – Moustier, say – and then all the others follow him!'

'Mélie, whatever are you waiting for? You ought to take out a patent at once. Why, it's pure genius. Is it your own invention, this method?'

'Lordy, no,' said Mélie, tucking some faded, fair wisps back under her coif. '*Everyone* knows it.

'Is that all the news?'

'No. Old Cagnat, my cousin, is so bad with his kidneys, that's he completely omnipotent.'

'He is, is he?'

'Deary me, yes. His legs have swelled right up to the knees, and what with having an intruding stomach too, he's quite capable, so to speak. What else? The new owners of the château at Pont de l'Orme are turning their park upside down to go in for apisiculture in a big way.'

'Pisciculture? But there isn't any water at Pont de l'Orme, is there?'

'It's funny how hard of hearing you are today, my poor girl! I tell you they're building lots and lots of hives so as to go in for apisiculture, there!'

As she was trimming a lamp, Mélie threw me a glance of affectionate contempt. Her vocabulary is full of surprises. One just needs to be on the alert.

It's hot in this hateful Paris! I don't want it to be hot! It isn't the fiery heat, fanned with cool breezes one breathes *there* without too much difficulty but a mugginess that oppresses me. Lying on my bed, in the afternoon, I think about far too many things, about Marcel who's forgotten me, about my cousin Uncle who's gallivanting about. He's disappointed me. Why was he so kind, so communicative, so almost affectionate with me, if he meant to forget me straight away? It would only have needed a few days, a few words, for us to have been completely at ease with each other and we could have gone out together often. I should like to have got to know the Paris world better with him. But he was a charming bad lot who wouldn't find Claudine adequate as a friend.

The lilies-of-the-valley on the chimneypiece intoxicated me and gave me a migraine. What was the matter with me? My unhappiness over Luce, yes, but something else too – my heart was aching with homesickness. I felt as ridiculous as that sentimental engraving hanging on the wall of Mademoiselle's drawing-room, *Mignon regretting her fatherland*. And I thought I was cured of so many things and had lost so many of my illusions! Alas, my mind kept going back to Montigny. Oh, to clasp armfuls of tall, cool grass, to fall asleep, exhausted, on a low wall hot from the sun, to drink out of nasturtium leaves, where the rain rolls like quicksilver, to

117

ransack the water's edge for forget-me-nots for the pleasure of letting them fade on a table, and lick the sticky sap from a peeled willow-wand; to make flutes of hollow grass-stalks, to steal tit's eggs and rub the scented leaves of wild currants; to kiss, to kiss all those things I love! I wanted to kiss a beautiful tree and the beautiful tree to kiss me back. - 'Go for a walk, Claudine, take some exercise.'

I can't go for a walk and I won't; it bores me! I prefer to stay at home and get feverish. Do you imagine they smell good, your Paris streets under the sun? And to whom can I tell everything that's weighing on my heart? Marcel would take me off to look at the shops to comfort me. His father would understand me better, but it would frighten me to show him so much of myself. The dark blue eyes of my cousin Uncle seem to guess so many things already, his beautiful, disturbing eyes with the bistred, wrinkled eyelids that inspire confidence – yet, at the very moment when that look says: 'You can tell me everything', a smile, below the silvering moustache, suddenly makes me uneasy. And Papa . . . Papa is working with Monsieur Maria. (Monsieur Maria's beard must make him hot, in this weather. Does he do it up in a little plait at night?)

How I've degenerated since last year! I've lost the innocent pleasure of running about and climbing and jumping like Fanchette. Fanchette doesn't dance any more because of her heavy stomach. I've got a heavy head, but luckily, I haven't any stomach.

I read, I read, I read. Everything. It doesn't matter what. I've nothing but that to occupy me, to take me away from here and from myself. I've no more homework to do. And if I no longer explain, at least twice a year, in a school essay why 'Idleness if the mother of all the vices', I understand far better now how it engenders some of them.

TWELVE

ON SUNDAY, I went back to see Aunt Wilhelmine, as it was her 'at-home-day'.

The omnibus passed in front of the block of flats where Luce lived. I was afraid of running into her. She would not have hesitated to make a tearful scene in public and my nerves felt none too strong.

My aunt, deflated by the heat, abandoned her 'at-home', and was slightly surprised by my visit. I did not make much elegant conversation.

'Aunt, things aren't going a bit well. I want to go back to Montigny, I'm fretting in Paris.'

'My child, you certainly don't look very well and your eyes are far too bright. Why don't you come and see me more often? You father, I won't so much as mention him. He's incurable.'

'I don't come because I'm bad-tempered and irritated with everything. I'd only hurt you, I'm only too capable of doing that.'

'Isn't that surely what they call homesickness? If only Marcel were here! But that secretive little thing probably never told you he was spending the day in the country?'

'He's jolly sensible, he'll see some leaves. Is he all alone? Doesn't that worry you, Aunt?'

'Oh, no,' she said, with that sweet smile of hers that hardly ever varied, 'he's gone off with his friend Charlie.'

'Oh, in that case,' I said, getting up suddenly from my chair, 'he's in good hands.'

Decidedly, this old lady was rather stupid; it wasn't to her either that I would make my confidences and moan that I felt like an uprooted tree. I shifted from one foot to the other, pining to go; she held me back, looking a trifle anxious.

'Would you like to see my doctor? An old doctor, very clever and experienced, in whom I have complete faith?'

'No, I don't want to. He'll tell me to distract myself, and to see people, and to make friends with girls of my own age. Girls of my own age, they're contemptible!'

All the same, that filthy Luce . . .

'Good-bye, Aunt. If Marcel can come and see me, I'd like that.' And I added, to soften my rudeness, 'He's the only friend of my own age I have.'

Aunt Coeur let me go, this time without attempting to stop me. I had disturbed the placidity of a blind, doting grandmother. Marcel was so much easier to bring up.

Aha, so they were seeking coolness under the trees, on the outskirts of the city, those two pretty boys! The greenness would be making them feel amorous, brightening their cheeks, turning Marcel's blue eyes to aquamarine and lightening the black eyes of his dear friend. It would be gloriously funny if they got caught together! Lord, how I should enjoy myself! But they knew their way about, they wouldn't get caught. They would come back by one of the evening trains, arm in arm, and separate with eloquent eyes. And I – I should be as I was now, all alone. Shame on you, Claudine! Isn't it ever going to stop, this obsession, this anguish of loneliness? All alone, all alone! Claire's getting married, I'm left all alone. Well, my dear, it's your own fault. So stay alone – with your virtue intact.

Yes. But I'm a poor, unhappy girl who takes refuge at night in Fanchette's soft fur and buries her hot mouth and her black-ringed eyes in it. I swear, I absolutely swear, all this can't be just the boring nervous edginess of a female who needs a husband. *I* need far, far more than a husband.

Thirteen

MARCEL HAS REAPPEARED. Today as the finishing touch to his grey suit – of a grey a turtle dove might envy – he wore an astonishing buttercup-yellow *crêpe-de-Chine* cravat. It was folded round the white collar of which only a narrow rim could be seen and draped in front and fastened with pearl-headed pins, like a woman's. I congratulated him on this find.

'Have a nice walk on Sunday?'

'Ah! Grandmother told you? That Grandmother of mine will end up by compromising me! Yes, an exquisite walk. Such weather!'

'And such a friend!'

'Yes,' he said, his eyes far away. 'A friend who matched the weather.'

'It's a second honeymoon, then?'

'Why *second*, Claudine?'

He was in a dreamy, melting mood, looking tired, yet enchanting, his eyelids mauve under his blue eyes. He seemed ready to drop all reserve and make unlimited confidences.

'Tell me about the walk.'

'The walk? Nothing to tell about it. We lunched at an inn on the river bank like two . . .'

'. . . lovers.'

'– drank some *vin rosé*,' he went on, without making any protest, 'and ate some fried potatoes, and after that there's really nothing to tell. We wandered about on the grass, in the shade. Honestly, I don't know what there was about Charlie that day, he *had* something.'

121

'He had you, that's all.'

Surprised at the tone of my voice, Marcel raised his languid eyes and looked at me.

'What an odd face you have, Claudine! A little anxious, pointed face – charming all the same. Your eyes have got bigger since the other day. Are you ill?

'Yes and no . . . troubles you wouldn't understand. And also something you would understand. I've seen Luce again.'

'Ah!' he cried, clasping his hands in a childish gesture. 'Where is she?'

'In Paris. She's here indefinitely.'

'And . . . so that's why you're looking so tired, Claudine! Oh, Claudine, what can I do to make you tell me all?'

'Nothing. It won't take long. I met her by chance. Yes, honestly, by chance. She took me home with her. Luxury fittings and furniture, a dress that cost thirty louis. Don't look startled, old boy!' I said, laughing at his half-open mouth that looked like a surprised baby's. 'And then, just as in the old days, she was the loving – too loving – Luce, her arms round my neck, her scent all round me, the over-trusting Luce who told me everything. Marcel, my friend, she's living in Paris with an old gentleman, she's his mistress.'

'Oh!' he exclaimed, with genuine indignation. 'How terribly that must have hurt you!'

'Not as much as I'd expected. A little, all the same.'

'My poor little Claudine!' he said throwing his gloves on my bed. 'I do understand so well.'

In an affectionate, brotherly way, he put his arm round my waist, and, with his free hand, drew my head against him. Were we touching or ridiculous? At that moment, I didn't stop to ask myself. He had his arm round my neck, like Luce. He smelt nice, like her, but of a subtler scent, and, looking up, I could see his fair eyelashes drooping like a shade over his eyes. Was all my nervous tension of that week going to burst into a storm of sobs then and there? No, he would dry my tears, that would wet his well-cut jacket, with a furtive uneasiness. I forced myself to bite my tongue vigorously, a sovereign remedy against impending tears.

'My little Marcel, you're sweet. It's been a comfort seeing you.'

'Be quiet. I understand so well. God! If Charlie did such a thing to me!'

Quite pink with selfish emotion, he mopped his temples. What he said struck me as so funny that I burst out laughing.

'Yes, your nerves are all to pieces. Let's go out, shall we? It's been raining and the temperature is quite bearable now.'

'Oh yes, do let's go out. That'll calm me down.'

'But tell me more. Was she very pressing, did she implore you?'

It never occurred to him for a moment that his insistence would be cruel if one were really suffering; he was trying to get something out of this for himself – what? A rather interesting new sensation.

'Yes, extremely pressing. I ran away, so as not to see her up there, in tears, with her blouse undone over her white skin, calling to me over the banisters to come back . . .'

My 'nephew' was breathing faster. No doubt this unduly early heat in Paris must be very exhausting.

I left him for a moment and returned wearing the boater I'm so fond of. Marcel, with his forehead against the window-pane, was looking out into the courtyard.

'Where shall we go?'

'Anywhere you like, Claudine, any old where. We'll go and have some iced tea with lemon to revive us. So . . . you won't ever see her again?'

'Never,' I said very firmly.

My companion heaved a great sigh. Perhaps he wished my jealousy had been less adamant, so that there would have been further anecdotes.

'We must tell Papa we're going out, Marcel. Come with me.'

Papa was in bliss, striding up and down his room and dictating things to Monsieur Maria. The latter raised his head, looked hard at me, looked hard at Marcel, and became gloomy. My noble father's broad shoulders, clad in a waisted frock-coat whose pockets were torn, were raised to their fullest extent to express his contempt for Marcel. Marcel returned the contempt in full but behaved with extreme deference.

'Run along, children. Don't be out long. Keep out of draughts. Bring me back some foolscap, the biggest size you can find, and some socks.'

'I brought three quires of foolscap in with me this morning,' put in Monsieur Maria, in a mild voice. He had not take his eyes off me for a moment.

'Splendid. All the same . . . one can never buy too much foolscap.'

We went off and I heard Papa, behind the closed door, burst into a haunting-song at the top of his voice.

> 'You should just see my thing,
> It would give you a start,
> It's a fine rosy pink
> Like an artichoke's heart.'

'He knows some very odd songs, my great-uncle,' observed Marcel, more astonished than ever.

'Yes. He and Mélie between them have a pretty complete repertoire. What always puzzles me is that "fine rosy pink like an artichoke's heart". Artichokes with crimson hearts are an unknown species, in Montigny, anyway.'

We walked fast so as to get away from the reeking Rue Jacob and the evil-smelling Rue Bonaparte. On the quays one could at last breathe, but here the breath of May smells of asphalt and creosote, alas!

'Where are we going?'

'I don't know yet. You're pretty, you're very pretty today, Claudine. Your tobacco-coloured eyes have something anxious and appealing about them that I've never seen in them before.'

'Thank you.'

I, too, felt I was looking my best. The shop-windows told me so, even the very narrow ones in which I could only see one eye and a slice of cheek as I passed by. What a weathercock I am! How I had wept for my long hair, and yet this very morning I had cut off three centimetres of my short locks, so as to keep the 'curly shepherd-boy' effect. *That's* an expression of my uncle's. The fact is that no other way of wearing my hair could make a better frame for my long eyes and my narrow chin.

People looked at us a good deal, at Marcel quite as much as at me, perhaps he was slightly embarrassing in the full glare of the streets. He kept laughing shrilly, and pivoting round on his hips to see his reflection in shop-windows and lowering his eyelids when men stared at him: these airs and graces of his left me decidedly cold.

'Claudinette, come and have some iced tea in the Boulevard Haussmann. Do you mind if we take the first boulevard to the right after the Avenue de l'Opera? It's more amusing.'

'No streets in Paris amuse *me*. It's so dull walking on the flat all the time. I say, do you know whether your father is back in Paris yet?'

'He hasn't informed me to that effect, dear. Papa goes about a lot. Journalism, "affairs of honour, affairs of the heart". You must know that my father is tremendously fond of women, and vice versa,' he said, over-emphatically, with the acid voice he used when he speaks of my cousin Uncle. 'Does that surprise you?'

'No, it doesn't surprise me. One out of two – that's not excessive for one family.'

'You're charming when you're annoyed, Claudine.'

'My little Marcel, do you honestly think I care a fig one way or the other?'

For it was essential to prove that I could lie very convincingly and not to let him see how distressed and uneasy those last words of his had made me feel. I seriously considered withdrawing my confidence from my cousin Uncle. I didn't like the idea of telling my secrets to someone who would go and forget them with 'women'. Besides, it was disgusting! I could hear that Uncle talking to 'women' in that same veiled, seductive voice, the voice that had said such charming, affectionate things to me. When his 'women' were unhappy, did he put his arm round their shoulders to comfort them, as he comforted me, three weeks ago? Oh, *damn*!

Claudine's utterly unreasonable irritation expressed itself

by shoving her elbow against the hip of a fat lady who was blocking her path.

'Whatever's the matter with you, Claudine?'

'Oh, shut up, *do*!'

'Temper, temper! Sorry, Claudine, I'd forgotten about your trouble. I know just what you're thinking of.'

His mind was still running on Luce. His misunderstanding restored my good temper a little. I felt like an unfaithful wife who had been deceived by her lover and who was being comforted by her husband.

Both of us deep in thoughts that we could not tell each other, we reached the Vaudeville. Suddenly, a voice – which I heard even before it uttered a word – whispered to my back: 'Good afternoon, model children.'

I swung round violently, my eyes blazing, bristling so much that my cousin Uncle burst out laughing. There he was, with another gentleman whom I recognized as Maugis of the concert. Maugis of the concert, plump and pink, was very hot. He mopped his forehead and bowed with an exaggerated deference that I suspected was mocking and that did not help to pacify me.

I stared at Uncle Renaud as if I were seeing him for the first time. His short arched nose and his moustache, the colour of a silvery beaver, were just as I remembered, but had his deep, tired blue-grey eyes changed their expression? I had not realized that his mouth was so small. The sharply-etched little lines on his temples ran right down to the corners of his eyes, but I did not find that altogether unattractive. Ugh! The horrible rake who had just come back from seeing his 'women'! And I studied him for those two seconds with such a vindictive expression that the loathsome Maugis was impelled to remark, shaking his head:

'Now *there's* a face I wouldn't allow to have any pudding . . . without further pretext.'

I shot him a glance with intent to kill, but his bulbous blue eyes and his arched eyebrows shammed such an expression of oily sweetness and total innocence that I laughed outright in his face . . . without further pretext.

'These old ladies,' observed the abominable Uncle,

shrugging his shoulders, 'they laugh at the merest trifle.'

I did not answer; I did not even look at him.

'Marcel, what's the matter with your girl friend? Have you two been quarrelling?'

'No, Father, we couldn't be better friends. But,' he added, with an air of knowledgeable discretion, 'I think Claudine has had some worries this week.'

'Don't fret yourself too much,' insisted Maugis. 'Dolls heads can easily be replaced. I know an excellent place . . . I can get them for you by the baker's dozen and five per cent. discount for cash.'

It was my uncle's turn now to look at me as if he were seeing me for the first time. He signed rather imperiously to Marcel to come and speak to him. As the two of them moved a step or two away, I was left to the mercy of the plump Maugis. He quite amuses me; he's never subtle but he's occasionally funny.

'He's looking his best today, the young man whose aunt you claim to be.'

'He certainly is! People stare at him in the street more than they do at me! But I'm not jealous.'

'How right you are!'

'He's wearing a lovely cravat, isn't he? But it's really a cravat for a woman.'

'Come, come, don't reproach him for having *something* for a woman,' said the Maugis placatingly.

'And his clothes . . . not one wrinkle to be seen!'

Surely, Marcel could not be telling his father about Luce? No, he wouldn't dare. He'd better *not* dare. No, if he had, my uncle's face would be looking quite different.

'Claudine,' he said, returning to us, with his son: 'I'd like to take you both to see *Blanchette* next Sunday at the Antoine theatre. But, if you're sulking, what am I to do? Go all alone?'

'No, not all alone, I'll come!'

'And bring your bad temper with you?'

He looked right into my eyes, and I gave in.

'No, I'll be nice. But I've got things on my mind today.'

He went on looking at me searchingly; he was trying to guess what was wrong. I turned my head away as Fanchette does from the saucer of milk she both wants and refuses.

'There, I'll leave you now, model children. Where are you off to like that?'

'We're going to have some iced tea, Father.'

'That's better than going to a pub,' muttered Maugis absently.

'Listen, Claudine,' my uncle said in my ear. 'I find Marcel very much easier to get on with since you and he have been friends. I think you're a good influence on him, little girl. His old Papa is extraordinarily grateful to you, do you know that?'

I let the two men shake hands with me and we turned our backs to them. A good influence on Marcel? That was something that left me completely cold! Moralizing isn't in my line. A good influence on Marcel? Oh Lord, what an utter fool an intelligent man can be!

We drank our iced tea with lemon. But my 'nephew' found me depressing company. I amuse him less than Charlie does, and I realize, moreover, that my own diversions are of an entirely different kind. It's not my fault, I can't help it.

Fourteen

THAT NIGHT, AFTER dinner, I read vaguely and absent-mindedly while Papa smoked, occasionally bursting into song with one of his barbarous ditties, and Mélie wandered about, weighing her breasts. The cat, swollen and enormous, had refused her dinner; she kept purring for no reason and her nose was too pink and her ears hot.

I went to bed late with the window open and the shutters closed, after going through my complicated routine. As usual, I washed all over in hot water, studied myself naked in the long-glass, did my limbering-up exercises. I felt limp and flat. My Fanchette, panting for breath, lay on her side in her basket, trembling and listening to her swollen stomach. I thought it would be soon now.

It certainly was soon! I had hardly blown out my lamp before a loud, despairing *miaooooo* made me leap out of bed. I lit the lamp again and ran, barefoot, to my poor little darling, who was breathing very fast. She put her hot paws imperiously on my hand and looked at me with beautiful, dilated eyes. She was purring wildly, without rhyme or reason. Suddenly, the delicate paws clenched on my hands and there was a second *miaoooo* of distress. Ought I to call Mélie? But, at the first movement I made to get up, Fanchette frantically got up too and tried to run; she was crazy with terror. The only thing to do was to stay. It disgusted me rather, but I wouldn't look.

After a ten minutes calm, the situation became acute. There were swift alternations of furious purring (*frrrr-frrrr*) and terrible cries (*miaoooo, miaooooo*). Fanchette's eyes nearly bolted from her head, a spasm convulsed her and . . . I turned away my head. Then the purring resumed and a stirring in the basked informed me that there was something new in it. But I knew only too well that the poor sweet never stopped at one. The cries broke out again, the frantic paw scratched my hand; I kept my head obstinately averted. After three such episodes, at last there was definite calm. Fanchette was empty. I rushed to the kitchen in my nightdress to get her some milk; that would give her time to tidy up all sorts of little things. I delayed, on purpose. When I returned with the saucer, my pretty, exhausted cat was already wearing her 'happy mother' face. I thought I might look now.

On the white and pink stomach, three minute kittens, three grey slugs with black stripes, three little marvels were sucking and wriggling like leeches. The basket was clean, without any trace left: Fanchette has the gift of having kittens as if by magic! I didn't dare touch the little things yet – they were shining from being licked from ear to tail though the little mother invited me in her poor, cracked voice to admire them, to stroke them. Tomorrow, we shall have to choose and have two of them drowned. Mélie, as usual, will be the Lord high Executioner. And for weeks I shall watch Fanchette being a capricious mother, carrying her striped little one about in her mouth, tossing him up in the air with her paws and being astonished, the incorrigible innocent, that this fortnight-old son doesn't jump up after her on to the chimneypiece and on to the top shelf of the book-case.

My shortened night was full of dreams, in which the extravagant vied with the idiotic. For some time, I've been dreaming more than usual. Mélie wept all the ready tears of her tender soul when she received the order to drown two of the little Fanchets. It was necessary to choose and to distinguish the sexes. Personally, I've no idea when they're so little and it seems that people more expert than I am make mistakes, but Mélie is infallible. A kitten in each hand, she gave one sure glance at the right place and declared:

'This one's the little male. The two others are shes.' I restored the little chosen one to Fanchette, who stood on the floor, mewing anxiously. 'Take the two others away quick, so that she won't know.' All the same, Fanchette did know some were missing; she can count up to three. But this enchanting animal showed up as a rather indifferent mother. After having roughly rolled her tom-kitten over with her paws and her nose to see if the others weren't hidden underneath him, she made up her mind. She would lick that one twice more, that was all.

How many days are there still to go? Four more till Sunday. On Sunday I'm going to the theatre with Marcel and my uncle. I'm indifferent about the theatre; about my uncle, no. My uncle, my uncle . . . What an idiotic notion to have christened him that! Silly mutt of a Claudine! 'My uncle' – it makes me think of that horrible little Luce. It doesn't worry her in the least to call *him* 'my uncle', that old gentleman who . . . This one, *mine*, in actual fact, is the widower of a first cousin whom I never even set eyes on. In plain French, that's called a cousin. 'Renaud' is better than 'Uncle', it makes him seem younger, it sounds right. Renaud! How quickly he conquered my bad temper, the other day. It was pure cowardice on my part, not courtesy. Obeying, obeying, that's a humiliation I've never endured – I was going to write 'savoured'. Yes, 'savoured'. It was out of perversity that I gave in, I believe. At Montigny, I'd have let myself be chopped up into small bits sooner than take my turn at sweeping the classroom if I didn't feel like it. But, perhaps, if Mademoiselle had given me a long look with grey-blue Renaud-coloured eyes, I might have obeyed more often, just as I obeyed *him*, all my limbs numb with a new, unknown weakness.

For the first time, I have just been able to smile at the thought of Luce. A good sign: she is becoming remote to me, this little thing who hopped about on one foot as she talked about letting her mother starve to death! . . . She doesn't know; it isn't her fault. She's just a little, velvety animal.

Still two more days before going to the theatre. Marcel is coming too. It isn't the thought of his presence that delights me most; when his father is there, he's a pink and golden little duffer, a slightly hostile little duffer. I like them better separately, Renaud and Marcel.

My mood – and why shouldn't I have 'moods' like anyone else – isn't easy to define clearly. It's the mood of someone who expects that, at any moment, a chimney may fall on their head. I live with my nerves strung up, waiting for this inevitable fall. And when I open the door of a cupboard, or when I turn the corner of a street, or when the post comes in the morning – the post that never brings me anything – my heart gives a slight jump. 'Is it going to happen *this* time?'

It's no good staring at the features of my little slug – he's called Limaçon, the kitten, to please Papa and also because he's much more like a snail than a slug, with his beautiful, clearly-marked stripes – it's no good looking inquiringly at his little closed face, raved with fine lines that converge towards the nose like the face of a yellow and black pansy, the eyes won't open till nine full days have gone by. And whenever I give white Fanchette back her beautiful child, paying her a thousand compliments she washes him meticulously. Though she loves me to distraction, she privately thinks that I smell horribly of scented soap.

Something has occurred; something really serious! Was it the chimney I was expecting to fall? Probably it was, but, in that case, I ought to feel relieved of my anxious apprehension. Whereas I've still got 'shrunk stomach' as they say in Montigny. This is what happened.

This morning, at ten o'clock, when I was assiduously trying to get Limaçon used to another of Fanchette's teats (he always takes the same one and, in spite of what Mélie says, I am afraid that may deform my lovely cat), Papa came into my room, looking very solemn. It wasn't seeing him look solemn that alarmed me, but seeing him come into my bedroom. He never enters it unless I announce that I'm ill.

'Come along with me for a moment.'

I followed him into his book-lair with the meekness of an inquisitive daughter. There I found Monsieur Maria. The mere fact of his being there seemed perfectly normal. But

Monsieur Maria, dressed in a brand-new frock-coat at ten o'clock in the morning and wearing gloves – that went beyond the bounds of reasonable possibility!

'My child,' began my noble father, with dignified unction, 'here is an excellent young man who wishes to marry you. I must tell you at the outset that he has my warmest approval.'

I listened with all my ears, attentive but stupefied. When Papa had finished his sentence, I articulated just one idiotic, but sincere word: 'What?'

I swear I really hadn't understood. Papa lost a little of his solemnity, but retained all his nobleness.

'Of all the bally idiots! Surely I articulate clearly enough for you to understand without having to repeat myself! This excellent little Monsieur Maria wants to marry you – if necessary, in a year's time, if you're too young. You know, I've rather tended to forget your exact age lately (!). I told him you must be quite fourteen and a half but he declares that you are going on for eighteen; he probably knows better than I. There! And if you don't want him, ten thousand herds of swine, you're hard to please!'

This was superb! I looked at Monsieur Maria, who turned pale beneath his beard and gazed at me with his long-lashed animal eyes. Suddenly feeling extraordinarily light-hearted, without quite knowing why, I darted up to Monsieur Maria.

'You mean it's true, Monsieur Maria? You really and truly want to marry me? You're not joking?'

'Oh! I'm not joking,' he said in a low, pathetic voice.

'How terribly, terribly nice of you!'

And I seized both his hands and shook them joyously. He turned crimson, like a setting sun behind a bushy wood.

'So . . . you consent, Mademoiselle?'

'Me? Not on your life!'

Ah! I had been about as tactful as a ton of dynamite! Monsieur Maria stood facing me with his mouth open, obviously feeling he must be going mad.

Papa thought it was his duty to intervene.

'Look here, are you going to keep us in suspense much longer? What does all this mean? First you fling yourself round his neck, then you refuse him. Extraordinary behaviour, I must say!'

'But, Papa, I don't in the least want to marry Monsieur Maria, that's quite definite. I think he's very nice – oh, terribly nice! – to think I'm worthy of such . . . such serious intentions, and that's what I'm thanking him for. But of course, I don't want to *marry* him!'

Monsieur Maria made a faint, pitiful, imploring gesture, but said nothing. He made me feel a brute.

'Eternal Father in heaven!' roared Papa. 'Why the devil don't you want to marry him?' Why? Spreading out both hands, I shrugged my shoulders. Had I any idea why? It was as if they were proposing I should marry Rabastens, the handsome assistant master at Montigny. Why? For the only valid reason in the world – because I didn't love him.

Papa, exasperated, launched into such a resounding volley of oaths that I couldn't attempt to write them down. I waited for the litany to come to an end.

'Oh, Papa! Do you want me to be unhappy then?'

That man of stone did not insist further.

'Idiot child! Unhappy? Of course not. Besides, anyway, you can think things over, you may change your mind. You there, Maria, she may change her mind, mayn't she? Actually, it would be extraordinarily convenient for me if she *did*! I'd have you here all the time and we'd really get on with the job! But, for this morning, positively for the last time, you *don't* want him? Then b—- off, we've got work to do!'

Monsieur Maria knew very well that I shouldn't change my mind. He fidgeted with his leather brief-case and searched for his pen without seeing it. I went up to him.

'Monsieur Maria, are you angry with me?'

'Oh no, Mademoiselle, it's not that . . .'

A sudden hoarseness prevented him from going on. I went away on tiptoe, and, alone in the drawing-room, I began to dance a fandango. What marvellous luck! Someone had asked for my hand in marriage! In *marriage*! Someone had thought me pretty enough, in spite of my short hair, to marry. And a sensible young man, too, who knew his own mind, not a pathological case. So, there might be others . . . Having danced enough, I decided to think of the future.

It would have been childish to deny it, my life was approaching a crisis. The chimney was imminent. It was going to fall on my whirling head; the result might be terrifying or delicious, but fall it inexorably would. I did not feel the slightest need to confide my situation to anyone else in the world. I should not write to Claire, happy Claire: 'Oh, dear little friend of my childhood, it is approaching fast, the fateful moment when I foresee that my heart and my life will burst into flower together,' I shall not ask Papa: 'Oh father mine, what can this be that both oppresses and delights me? Englighten my young ignorance.' . . . He'd only pull a long face, poor Papa! He would twist his tri-coloured beard and mutter perplexedly: 'I've never studied that particular species.'

Come off it, Claudine, come down to earth . . . In your heart of hearts, you're conceited. You wander about the enormous flat, you desert your beloved old Balzac, you stop with a lost, vague look in front of your bedroom glass that shows you a tall slim girl with her hands clasped behind her back, in a red silk pleated blouse, and a dark blue serge skirt. She has short hair in big curls, a narrow face with warm ivory cheeks, and long eyes. You think she's pretty, that girl, who looks as if she didn't care a rap for anyone or anything. It's not a beauty that excites the mob but . . . I've definitely got *something*: those who can't see it are either idiots or short-sighted.

I simply *must* look my best tomorrow! My blue coat and skirt will do, and my big black hat, with the little dark blue silk blouse – dark colours suit me best – and two tea-roses tucked into the corner of its square neck, because, at night, they're exactly the same colour as my skin.

Shall I tell Mélie that I've had a proposal of marriage? No, it's not worth it. She'd only answer, 'My lamby, you should do as we do at home. Them as proposes to you, try them out first. That way, all's fair and square and no one gets a bad bargain.' For her, virginity is something quite worthless. I know her theories. 'All a pack of lies, my poor girl! Nothing but a lot of doctors' faddy notions. Before, after, don't you go

135

imagining the men aren't every bit as keen! Go on with you, it's all one to *them*!' Well, I've no lack of good instruction! But decent girls are doomed by fate; they remain decent in spite of all the Mélies in the world!

I got to sleep late, that stifling night. Memories of Montigny drifted through my troubled sleep; thoughts of rustling leaves, of the chilly dawn, of mounting larks with that song we used to imitate at the School by rubbing a handful of glass marbles together. Tomorrow, tomorrow . . . would someone else think me pretty? Fanchette purred softly, her striped Limaçon between her paws. How often my beautiful darling's even purr has soothed me and sent me to sleep.

I dreamed that night. And when the plump, flabby Mélie came in at eight to open my shutters she found me sitting huddled up in a ball with my knees in my arms and my hair over my nose, taciturn and preoccupied.

'Good morning, my precious pet!'

'. . . 'morning.'

'You're not ill?'

'No.'

'Got worries and troubles?'

'No. I had a dream.'

'Ah, that's ever so much more serious. Still if you didn't dream a child nor the royal family (*sic*), there's no harm done. If only you'd dream a man's dung, now!'

These predictions, which she had solemnly repeated to me ever since I could understand what she said, didn't seem funny any more. What I *did* dream, I will never tell anyone, not even this exercise book. It would embarrass me too much to see it in writing.

I had asked that we should have dinner at six o'clock, and Monsieur Maria, self-effacing as usual, went off an hour early, eclipsed in his bushy beard, and looking dejected. I have not avoided him at all since the Event; he doesn't embarrass me in the least. I have even been more forthcoming than usual; full of bright, chatty commonplaces.

'What lovely weather, Monsieur Maria!'

'Do you think so, Mademoiselle? It's very oppressive, the west looks black . . .'

'Ah, I hadn't noticed. It's funny, ever since this morning I've been imaging it was fine.'

At dinner, as I was lingering over the jam soufflé after having toyed with my meat with no appetite, I asked Papa a question. 'Papa, have I got a dowry?'

'Why the hell d'you want to know that?'

'Honestly, you're marvellous! Someone proposed to me yesterday, it might happen again tomorrow. It's only the first refusal that's difficult. You know, proposals are like the old story of the ants and the pot of jam; when one comes along, so do three thousand more.'

'Good Lord, three thousand! Mercifully we haven't a vast number of acquaintances. Certainly, pot of jam, you possess a dowry! When you made your First Communion, I put them in charge of Meunier, the solicitor at Montigny, your hundred and fifty thousand francs. They were left you by your mother, a remarkably unpleasant woman. They're safer with him than here, you know, with me, one never knows what might happen.'

Now and then he says touching things like that that make you want to kiss him – and I did kiss him. Then I went back to my room, my nerves already on edge because it was getting late, listening for the sound of the bell with my ears strained and my heart limp.

Half past seven. He certainly wasn't hurrying himself! We should miss the first act! Supposing he wasn't going to come! A quarter to eight. It was revolting! He could at least have sent me a telegram, or even Marcel, this fugitive uncle.

But an imperious *trrr* made me leap to my feet and I saw, in the glass, a strange white face that embarrassed me so much that I averted my head. For some time now, my eyes have taken to looking as if they knew something I did not know myself. The voice I heard in the hall made me smile nervously; a single voice, that of my cousin Uncle – of my cousin Renaud, I should say. Mélie brought him straight in, without knocking at my door. Her eyes followed him with the flattering gaze of an obedient bitch. He was pale too and obviously on edge; his

137

eyes were glittering. In the artificial light, his silvery
moustache looked more golden. If I had dared, I would like to
have touched that beautiful, upturned moustache to feel how
soft it was.

'So you're all alone, Claudine! Why don't you say
something? Has Mademoiselle gone out?'

Mademoiselle was thinking that perhaps he had come
straight from one of his 'women' and smiled mirthlessly.

'No, Mademoiselle is just going out . . .with you I hope.
Come and say good-bye to Papa.'

Papa was charming to my cousin Uncle who is only
unattractive to women.

'Take good care of the child; she's delicate. Have you the
key to get in with?'

'Yes, I've got my own to get into my flat.'

'Ask Mélie to give you ours. I've already lost four, I give up.
What's happened to the little boy?'

'Marcel? He's not . . . he's meeting us at the theatre, I
believe.'

We went downstairs without saying a word. I was pleased
as a child to find a hansom waiting for us below. A coupé
from Binder's, drawn by magnificent horses, could not have
enchanted me more.

'Are you all right? Would you like me to pull up one of the
windows, because of the draught? No, I'll pull them both half
up, we'll be so hot otherwise.'

I'd no idea whether I was hot, but, heavens, how 'shrunk'
my stomach was! A nervous shiver made my teeth chatter; at
last I managed to say, with an effort:

'So Marcel's meeting us there?'

No reply. Renaud – how nice that was, just plain Renaud –
stared straight ahead, frowning. Suddenly, he turned to me
and seized my wrists; this man who was turning grey had such
young movements!

'Listen, I lied just now, that was rather mean of me. Marcel
isn't coming. I told your father he was and I'm vexed with
myself about that.'

'What? He's not coming? Why?'

'That's a disappointment for you, isn't it? It's my fault. His too. I don't know how to explain to you . . . It'll all seem to you so petty. He came to fetch me at my flat in the Rue Bassano, looking charming, with his little face less stiff and secretive than usual. But his tie! A *Crêpe-de-Chine* wound round his neck, draped like the tops of a woman's bodice, with pearl pins all over the place, frankly . . . impossible. I said: "My dear boy, would you do me a great favour and change your tie? I'll lend you one of mine." He took offence, became insolent and sarcastic and we . . . well, in the end we had a quarrel about something rather too involved to tell you, Claudine. He insisted: "I'll go in my cravat or I won't go at all." I slammed the door behind him, and that was that. Are you very angry with me?'

'But,' I said, ignoring the question, 'you've seen it already, that cravat. He was wearing it the other day when you met us, with Maugis, on the boulevard near the Vaudeville.'

He raised his eyebrows and looked extremely surprised.

'You don't say so! Are you sure?'

'Absolutely sure. It's a cravat you couldn't possibly forget. However was it you didn't notice it?'

Leaning back once more against the cushions, he shook his head and said in a rather subdued voice:

'I don't know. I noticed that you had circles round your eyes, and a wild, shy look like an offended deer. And a blue blouse, and a little wisp of curl that kept tickling your right eyebrow.'

I said nothing. I felt a little chokey. As he suddenly broke off what he was saying, he tilted his hat over his eyes with the curt gesture of a man who has just said something idiotic and realizes it too late.

'Obviously, it's dull for you, just me on my own. I can still take you home again if you'd rather, my dear.' To whom was that aggressive tone really addressed? I only laughed softly, laid my gloved hand on his arm and left it there.

'No, don't take me home. I'm very pleased. You don't get on together, you and Marcel. I prefer seeing you separately rather than together. But why didn't you say all this in front of Papa?'

He took my hand and tucked it under arm.

'Perfectly simple. I was hurt and annoyed, and I was frightened you father would deprive me of you, dear little compensation. I hadn't perhaps, deserved you but I had certainly earned you.'

'You'd nothing to be frightened about. Papa would have let me go off with you, he does everything I want.'

'Oh, I quite realize that,' he said, a little irritably, pulling his moustache that was like silver-gilt with the gold wearing off. 'Promise me, at least, that you'll always want such eminently reasonable things.'

'One never knows, one never knows! What I really *would* like . . . listen, grant me the thing I'm just going to ask you for.'

'What banana tree must I plunder? What fabulous artichoke must I strip to its heart? One word, one gesture, one single one . . . and your lap shall be filled with chocolate creams . . . These meagre hansom-cabs restrict the nobility of my gestures, Claudine, but not, I assure you, of my sentiments!'

All these literary men talk in the same, rather exaggerated, bantering way, but how much less elephantine he was than Maugis who had that horrible Paris working-class accent into the bargain.

'I've never been known to refuse chocolate creams. But . . . I don't want to call you "Uncle" any more. There, it's out!'

In the passing lights from a shop window, he bowed his head in mock resignation.

'It's come at last. She's going to call me "Grandfather". The dreaded hour has struck.'

'No, don't laugh. I've been thinking it over for a long time – that you're my cousin and that, if you didn't mind, I might call you . . . Renaud. I don't think it's such a monstrous request.'

We were driving up a dimly-lit avenue; he bent down to look at me; I made heroic efforts not to blink. At last he replied:

'Is that all? But begin at once, I implore you. You take years off my age, not as many as I could wish, but at least five already. Look at my temples – haven't they suddenly turned golden again?'

I leant forward to see, but, almost at once, I drew back again. Looking at him so close to made my stomach shrink almost to nothing.

We said no more. From time to time, as the lights came and went, I glanced furtively at his short profile and his eyes, wide open and alert.

'Where do you live . . . Renaud?'

'I told you, Rue de Bassano.'

'Is it pretty, your flat?'

'Well, it suits *me*.

'Could I see it?'

'Good Lord, no!'

'Why not?'

'Why, because . . . well . . . it's too . . . eighteenth-century engraving for you.'

'Pooh! What does *that* matter?'

'Let me have the illusion that these things do still matter a little. We're there, Claudine.'

'What a pity!'

Before *Blanchette*, I conscientiously enjoyed *Poil de carotte*. I was enchanted by Suzanne Després's boyish grace and restrained gestures: under the short red wig, her eyes were green, like Luce's. And Jules Renard's clear-cut, incisive dialogue delighted me too.

As I was listening, absolutely still, with my chin thrust forward, all at once I *felt* Renaud was looking at me. I turned my head swiftly' he had his eyes on the stage and an extremely innocent expression. That proved nothing.

During the interval, Renaud walked me about and inquired:

'Are you a trifle calmer now, you nervous little thing?'

'I wasn't nervous,' I said, bristling.

'And that delicate, tense little paw that felt so cold on my arm in the cab? Not nervous? Oh dear no, *I'm* the nervous one!'

'You are . . . too.'

I had spoken very low, but the faint pressure of his arm showed me that he understood.

During the performance of *Blanchette*, I found myself

141

thinking of the laments – how far they receded already – of Mademoiselle's little Aimée. In the days when we were beginning to be fond of each other, she used to confide to me – more crudely than that Blanchette in the play – the horrified aversion she had developed for her own home. The little teacher, already accustomed to the comparative comfort of the School, was revolted by the very thought of her parents' cottage and the whole poverty-stricken, ill-kept, squalling household. She used to tell me endlessly about her fears and miseries, standing in the doorway of the stinking classroom, and shivering like a little half-starved cat in the draught. And Mademoiselle would pass behind our backs, jealous and silent . . .

My neighbour, who seemed to be listening to my thoughts, asked me almost in a whisper:

'Is it like that in Montigny?'

'Like that, only much worse!'

He did not press me further. Elbow to elbow, we stayed silent; little by little, I relaxed against that kind, reassuring shoulder. At one moment, I lifted my head to him. His intelligent eyes looked down into mine and I smiled at him with all my heart. I have seen that man exactly five times; I have known him all my life.

When it came to the last act, I put my elbow down first and I left a little place on the velvet arm of the stall. His elbow understood perfectly and came to meet mine. I had entirely lost that shrinking sensation in my stomach.

At a quarter to midnight, we left the theatre. The sky was dark, the wind almost fresh.

'Please, Renaud, I don't want to get into a cab straight away. I'd must rather walk along the boulevards – have you got time?'

'My entire lifetime, if necessary,' he answered, smiling.

He held me by the arm, firmly, and we walked in step, because I have long legs. Under the electric lights, I could see us walking: Claudine had a strange, exalted little face turned upwards to the stars and her eyes were almost black; the wind streamed through Renaud's long moustache.

'Tell me about Montigny, Claudine, and about yourself.'

But I shook my head. It was perfect, as we were. There was no need to talk. We walked fast; I had Fanchette's paws tonight; the ground was like a springboard under my feet.

Lights, bright lights, coloured window-panes, people sitting at tables on a terrace, drinking.

'What's that?'

'It's the Brasserie Logre.'

'Oh, I'm so thirsty!'

'I'd like nothing better. But not in this Brasserie.'

'*Yes*, here, please! It's all lit up and exciting, it looks amusing.'

'But it's arty and tarty, not to mention noisy.'

'So much the better! I want to have a drink here.'

He pulled at his moustache for a second, then with a gesture that said: 'After all, why not?', he shepherded me into the main room. It was not so crowded as he had implied; in spite of the time of year, it was almost possible to breathe. The green tiled pillars awoke thoughts of baths and jugs of cool water.

'Thirsty! Thirsty!'

'There, there, keep calm, you shall have your drink! What a redoubtable child! It would be unwise to refuse *you* a husband.'

'I agree,' I said, unsmiling.

We were sitting at a little table against a pillar. To my right, under a panel daubed tempestuously with naked Bacchantes, a mirror assured me that I had no ink on my cheek, that my hat was on straight, and that my eyes were dancing above a mouth red with thirst, perhaps with a little fever. Renaud, sitting opposite me, had shaky hands and moist temples.

A little moan of covetousness escaped me, aroused by the trail of scent left by a passing dish of shrimps.

'Some shrimps too? Well, well! How many?'

'How many? I've never discovered how many I could eat. A dozen to begin with, after that we'll see.'

'And to drink, what? Beer?'

I made a face.

'Wine? No. Champagne? Asti Spumante?'

I flushed with greed.

'Oh! *Yes!*'

I waited impatiently and I watched several beautiful women come in, wearing light evening cloaks with sparkling embroideries. All very pretty – crazy hats, over-golden hair, flashing rings. My great friend, to whom I pointed out each new arrival, displayed an indifference that shocked me. Were 'his women' more beautiful, perhaps? I turned suddenly fierce and gloomy. He was surprised and started quoting edifying authors:

'What? The wind has turned? "Hilda, whence comes thy sorrow?"'

But I did not answer a word.

They brought the Asti. To drive away my care and to quench my thirst, I drank a big glass in one gulp. The womanizer opposite me excused himself for devouring red roast-beef on the grounds he was dying of hunger. The musky, treacherous fire of the Asti Spumante made the lobes of my ears begin to burn and my throat feel thirsty again. I held out my glass and, this time, I drank more slowly, my eyes half-closed with pleasure. My friend laughed:

'You drink like a baby at the breast. You've all the spontaneous grace of an animal, Claudine.'

'Fanchette has a son, you know.'

'No, I didn't know. You ought to have showed him to me! I bet he's as beautiful as a star.'

'Even more beautiful than that. Oh, these shrimps! If you only knew, Renaud' – each time I called him Renaud, he raised his eyes and looked at me – 'down there in Montigny, they're simply tiny . . . I used to go and pick them up with my hands, at Gué-Richard, paddling barefoot. These are simply marvellously seasoned.'

'You swear you won't be ill?'

'Good heavens, no! I was going to tell you something else, but something serious this time. Don't you think there's something extraordinary about me tonight?'

I thrust my face, rosy from the Asti, towards him. He leant forward too, and looked at me at such close quarters that I could see the fine wrinkles on his brownish eyelids; then he turned away, saying:

'No, not more tonight than the other times.'

'Then you're blind! My friend, the day before yesterday, as recently as that, at eleven o'clock in the morning, I had a pro-po-sal of marriage!'

'Hell's . . . who was the idiot who . . .'

Rapturous at the effect I had produced, I laughed out loud in ascending scales then stopped suddenly, because people at the other tables had heard and were looking round at us. Renaud was anything but rapturous.

'It's monstrous of you to lead me up the garden path! Of course, I didn't believe a word of it really.'

'I can't very well spit, can I? But I give you my word of honour, he *did* propose!'

'Who?'

That 'Who?' was anything but benevolent.

'An extremely nice young man – Monsieur Maria – Papa's secretary.'

'You refused him . . . naturally?'

'I refused him . . . naturally.'

He poured himself out a large glass of the Asti he disliked so much and ran his hand through his hair.

As for me, who never drank anything but water at home, I was observing some extraordinary phenomena. A kind of faint, misty trellis was rising from the table, making a halo round the lights and making objects seem very far away at one moment, and very close to the next.

At the moment when I was trying to analyse my sensations, a well-known voice bellowed from just inside the doorway:

'Kellner! Will you have the goodness to produce some Sauerkraut, mother of heart-burn and some of that insipid, salicylated cocoa that you have the impudence to denominate Munich beer. Liquid velvet, flowing perfumed locks of the Rheintochter, forgive them, they know not what they drink! "Weia, waga, waga la weia." . . .'

It was Maugis, lyrical and perspiring. Wagnerizing away at the top of his voice, with his flat-brimmed top hat on the back of his head and his waistcoat undone. He had three friends in tow. Renaud could not restrain a gesture of extreme annoyance and tugged his moustache, growling something under his breath,

As he came close to us, Maugis suddenly stopped his garglings from the *Rheingold*, opened his round protruding eyes wide, hesitated a moment, then raised his hand and passed on without greeting us.

'There!' muttered Renaued furiously.

'Whatever is it?'

'It's your fault, child. Most of all it's mine. You oughtn't to be here, alone with me. That imbecile Maugis . . . anyone would have done the same. Do you think there's any particular point in giving people wrong ideas about you, and about me?'

For one second, I was chilled by his vexed and worried eyes, but the next instant, I revived.

'Was *that* why? You don't mean you're making all that fuss and putting on all that performance of frowns and moral indignation just for *that*? But, I ask you, whatever harm can it do me? Give me something to drink . . . pleashe.'

'You don't understand! I'm not in the habit of taking respectable little girls out. A girl as pretty as you, alone with me, what do you expect people to suppose?'

'And what else?'

My drunken smile and my wandering eyes suddenly made it dawn on him.

'Claudine! You aren't, by any chance, a little . . . gay? You're drinking pretty hard tonight, do you at home?'

'At home I swig Évian water,' I replied in a kind, reassuring voice.

'Oh Lord! Now we're in a nice mess! What on earth am I going to say to your father?'

'He's gone to bye-byes.'

'Claudine, don't drink any more! Give me that full glass this minute!'

'Do you want me to hit you?'

Putting my glass out of reach of his prudent hands, I drank, and I listened to myself being happy. This was not altogether easy to do. The chandelier's misty haloes kept getting bigger and bigger like the halo round the moon when it's going to rain. 'The moon's drinking', as they say in Montigny. Perhaps, in Paris, it's a sign of rain when chandeliers drink! It's you, Claudine, who've been drinking. Three large glasses of Asti, you little 'wurzit'! How nice it is! It makes one's ears go *sshh, sshh*. The two gentlemen eating two tables away, did they really exist? Without moving, they came so close up that I could have sworn I only had to put out my hand to touch them. No, now they were ever so far away. Besides, there wasn't any space between objects; the chandeliers were stuck to the ceiling, the tables stuck to the walls, the fat gentlemen stuck to the light background of the glittering cloaks sitting further away. I exclaimed loudly:

'I understand! It's all in Japanese perspective!'

Renaud raised a despairing arm, then mopped his brow. In the glass to my right, I saw a most extraordinary Claudine with her hair in ruffled feathers, her long eyes full of delicious confusion, her lips bright and wet! That was the other Claudine, the one who had 'run past herself' as they say at home. And opposite her was that silver-streaked gentleman who kept looking at her and looking at her, who wasn't looking at anything *but* her and wasn't eating any more. Oh, I knew perfectly well! It wasn't the Asti, it wasn't the pepper in the shrimps that had intoxicated the little girl; it was that presence, it was that almost black gaze with the lights shining in it.

Completely two people now, I watched myself behaving, I heard myself talking, in a voice that seemed to come from rather far off, and the sensible Claudine, fettered and imprisoned in a glass cell, listened to the crazy Claudine chattering away and could do nothing for her. She couldn't do anything and, moreover, she didn't want to do anything. The chimney, whose collapse I had been dreading, had fallen with a great crash and the dust of its fall made a golden halo round the electric light bulbs. Help, sensible Claudine, above all, don't stir! The crazy Claudine is pursuing her course with the infallibility of the mad and the blind.

Claudine looked at Renaud: she fluttered her lashes, dazzled. Resigned, carried away, swept along in her wake, he sat silent, looking at her, one might say, with even more sorrow than pleasure. She burst out:

'Oh, how happy I am! O *you*, who didn't want to come! Aha, when I want something . . . We won't ever go away from here, will we? If you only knew! I obeyed you the other day, me, Claudine! I've never obeyed anyone except on purpose, before you . . . but obeying, in spite of yourself, when your knees feel nice and nasty at the same time – oh, that must be why Luce liked being beaten so much, you know, Luce? I used to beat her so much, without knowing she was perfectly right, she used to roll her head on the window-sill just where the wood's worn because, during recreations, we split cornies on it. Do you know too what "cornies" are? One day I wanted to fish for myself in the pond at Barres and I caught a fever, I was twelve and I had all my lovely hair. You'd like me better, wouldn't you, with my hair long? I've got "quivers" at the tips of my fingers, a whole "quiverful" -Do you smell that? A smell of absinthe? The fat gentleman's poured some into his champagne. At school we used to eat green barley sugar flavoured with absinthe; it was considered awfully smart to suck them for ages till they got a long point on them. That gawk Anaïs was so greedy and so patient that the little ones used to bring her their barley-sugars, "Make mine pointed!" they used to say. Disgusting, wasn't it? I dreamt about you. a wicked dream, too good to be true! But now I'm *somewhere* else, I don't in the least mind telling you . . .'

'Claudine!' he implored, very low.

The crazy Claudine, leaning towards him, with her two hands laid flat on the tablecloth, kept her eyes on his face. They were wild and held no secrets; a light, straying curl tickled her right eyebrow. She was talking as a vase overflows, this silent, reserved creature. She saw him turn red, then pale; she saw that he was breathing fast, and all this struck her as perfectly natural. But why did he not seem as ecstatic, as released from all constraint as she was herself? She dimly asked herself this vague question and answered herself aloud, with a sigh:

'Now, nothing sad can ever happen to me again.'

Renaud beckoned the head-waiter with the emphatic insistence of a man saying inwardly: 'Things can't go on like this.'

Claudine said irrelevantly, her cheeks burning, as she nibbled one of her tea-roses:

'How stupid you are.'

'Am I?'

'Yes. You've told a lie. You stopped Marcel from coming tonight on purpose.'

'No, Claudine.'

That very gentle 'no' struck home and sobered her a little. She let herself be put on her feet and drawn towards the door, like a little sleepwalker. Only the floor turned soft under her like asphalt that was still warm. Renaud only just had time to grasp her by one elbow; he guided her, almost carried her into the closed cab and sat down beside her. The cab drove off. With her head buzzing and almost completely blank, Claudine leant against the helpful shoulder. He became anxious.

'Are you feeling ill?'

No reply. Then:

'No. But hold me, because I'm swimming. Everything else is swimming, too. You're swimming too, aren't you?'

He wrapped his arm round her waist, sighing with apprehension. She leant her head against him, but her hat got in the way. She took it off with a fumbling hand and laid it on her lap, then once again she leant her head against the kind shoulder, with the blissful security of someone who has at last reached the end of a long journey. And the sensible Claudine looked on, observed, and gradually began to come closer. A lot of use, *she* was! She was very nearly as demented, that sensible Claudine, as the other one.

Her companion, her beloved friend, had not been able to stop himself from hugging the small body that lay so trustfully abandoned in his arms. He mastered himself and gave her a gentle shake:

'Claudine, Claudine, we're nearly there! Come to! Can you manage to get up the stairs?'

'What stairs?'

'Your stairs. The ones in the Rue Jacob.'

'You're going to leave me?'

She was sitting up straight now, stiffened like a snake.

149

Bareheaded and dishevelled, her panic-stricken face was one agonized question.

'But look, child, look! Come to your senses. We've both been idiots tonight. It's all my fault this has happened.'

'You're going to leave me!' she cried, heedless of the driver's attentive back, 'Where do you expect me to go? It's you I want to go with, it's you . . .'

Her eyes reddened and her mouth tightened. She almost screamed:

'Oh, I know! Go away, I know why you want to. You're going to your *women*, the ones you love. Marcel told me you had at least six of them! They don't love you – they'll leave you – they're ugly! You're going to sleep with them, every single one of them! And you'll kiss them, you'll even kiss them on the mouth! And who's going to kiss *me*? Oh! why don't you want me, at least for your daughter? I ought to have been your daughter, your friend, your wife – everything, everything!'

She flung herself on his neck and clung to it, weeping and sobbing.

'There's no one but you in the world, no one but you, and you're leaving me!'

Renaud wrapped her close in his arms; his mouth searched the curly nape, the warm neck, the cheeks salt with tears.

'Leaving you, my sweet, my adorable!'

She fell suddenly silent. She raised her wet face and looked at him with extraordinary intensity. He was panting and pale; his face was young, under the silvery hair; Claudine could feel the muscles trembling in the great arms that held her. He bent down to the little girl's hot mouth; she struggled and leant back, hardly knowing whether she was yielding herself or resisting. The sharp jolt of the cab against the pavement threw them apart, intoxicated, serious, and trembling.

'Good-bye, Claudine.'

'Good-bye.'

'I'm not coming up with you. I'll light your candle. You've got the key?'

'The key, yes.'

'I can't come and see you tomorrow; it's tomorrow already.

I'll come the day after tomorrow, for certain, at four o'clock.'

'At four o'clock.'

Meekly, she let him give her hand a long kiss, breathing in, as he bent over it, the faint smell of mild tobacco he carried about him. Then, like a dreamer awakened, she climbed the three flights and went to bed. In her four-poster the crazy Claudine was rejoined – high time too – by the sensible Claudine. But the sensible Claudine, respectful and admiring, timidly effaced herself before the other who had gone straight where Destiny had impelled her. She had marched forward, without once looking back, like a conqueror or someone on their way to the scaffold.

FIFTEEN

LANGUOR. LANGUOR ALL over. The delicious languor of someone who has been beaten or caressed almost to death. My calves were trembling, my hands were cold, there was a numb feeling in the nape of my neck. And my heart kept beating faster and faster, as if it wanted to catch up with the tick-tock of my little watch, then stopping and starting up again with a *Poum*! So this was true love, the real thing? Yes, because no place was bearable to me but his shoulder, where my lips almost touched his neck when I nestled against it. Then I smiled with pity at the mental image of Marcel's delicate cheeks against Renaud's wrinkled temples. Thank God, no, he wasn't young! Because of that noble, almost lunatic father of mine, I needed a Papa, I needed a friend, I needed a lover. Oh, heavens, a lover! It was hardly worth while having read so much and bragged about my erotic knowledge – entirely theoretical – if that mere word passing through my mind made me clench my teeth and curl up my toes. What should I do in his presence if I couldn't prevent myself from thinking? He would see, he would think about it too. Help, help! Suddenly, I felt dying of thirst.

The open window and the water in my jug helped a little. My candle was still burning on the chimneypiece. Looking at the glass, I was stupefied to see *that* was not more obvious. At four o'clock, in broad daylight, I fell asleep exhausted.

'Are you hungry, my lamb? You chocolate's been waiting for you since half past seven and it's going on nine, to be sure. Oh, oh what a face!'

'What's the matter with it?'

'Something's gone and changed my baby!'

Her sure old servant's instinct took in my tiredness, noticed the crumpled feathers of the hat flung on the chair, exulted in my headache. She got on my nerves.

'Have you finished weighing your breasts like melons? Which one's the ripest?'

But she laughed very softly and went off to her kitchen, singing one of her most outrageous songs:

> '*The Montigny girls*
> *Are as hot as live coals*
> *You're surely in luck*
> *When you . . .*'

I must confine myself to this brief quotation.

What had really woken me up was the terror of having only dreamt that whole impossible night.

Was *that* how tremendous things happened? Blessed be Asti and highly seasoned shrimps! Without them, I should certainly never have had the courage.

I might not have had the courage that particular evening, but, some other evening, my heart would have gone *humpetty-bump* just the same. But he loved me, didn't he? Hadn't he been pale? Wouldn't he have lost his head, like a simple Claudine, but for that unlucky – that lucky – no, I *mean*, but for that *unlucky* pavement in the Rue Jacob that caught the edge of the cab-wheel? No man had ever kissed me on the mouth. His was narrow and alive, with a round, firm lower lip. Oh, Claudine, Claudine, how you are turning into a child again as you feel yourself becoming a woman! As I conjured up his mouth and the passion in his darkened eyes, a delicious distress made me clasp my hands.

Other ideas assailed me too, but I did not in the least want to dwell on them at that moment.

'It certainly does hurt!' echoed Luce's sing-song voice. No, no: she had slept with a swine, that didn't prove anything! Besides, what did it matter? What mattered was that he

153

should be there all the time, that the dear place on his shoulder should always be there ready for me at every hour of the day and night, and that his great arms should shelter me every time they closed round me. My liberty oppressed me, my independence exhausted me; what I had been searching for for months – for far longer – I knew, with absolute clarity, was a master. Free women are not women at all. He would know all that I didn't know; he would rather despise all that I did know; he would call me 'My little silly!' and stroke my hair.

My dream was so vivdly real to me that, to reach up to *his* hand, I lowered my forehead and stood on tiptoe, like Fanchette when she wants me to scratch the top of her little flat skull. 'You have all the spontaneous grace of an animal, Claudine . . .' Lunchtime found me thoughtfully examining myself in a handglass, with my hair brushed back from my temples, wondering whether he would like my pointed ears.

Having quickly had enough of orange salad and fried potatoes, I left Papa alone with his coffee into which he daily methodically drops seven pieces of sugar and a morsel of pipe-ash. And I abandoned myself to bitter despair at the thought that I had twenty-seven hours to wait! Read? I couldn't, I could *not*! Strands of silvery-gold hair kept sweeping over the pages of the book. And I could not go out either; the streets swarmed with men whose name was not Renaud, and who would stare at me and try to make an impression on me, the imbeciles!

A small piece of stuff rolled up into a ball in my tub-chair managed to extract a smile from me. It was one of my little chemises, begun long ago! Sewing was the thing! Claudine would be needing chemises. Would Renaud like this one? White and filmy, with a charming little lace edge and white ribbon shoulder-straps . . . Some nights, when I feel particularly pleased with myself, I study myself in front of the glass in my chemise, a tall, slim little Madame Sans-Gêne with curls over her nose. Renaud *can't* find me ugly. Oh, heavens, I'd be so near, so much *too* near him in nothing but a thin chemise. My trembling hands sewed all crooked and, quite absurdly, I could hear the far-away voice of the favourite, the thin voice of Mademoiselle's little Aimée, at sewing lessons: 'Claudine, I implore you, *do* be more careful with your hemstitching. You're not getting it nice and even. Look at Anaïs's!'

Someone had rung the bell. Breathless, with my heart stopped, I listened, thimble in air. It was he, it was he, he hadn't been able to wait! Just as I was about to get up and run, Mélie knocked, and brought in Marcel.

Stupefaction made me remain seated. Marcel? That was someone I had completely forgotten! For several hours, he had been dead. What, Marcel! Why Marcel, not the other!

Supple and silent, he kissed my hand and sat down on the little chair. I stared at him with a dazed expression. He was rather pale, extremely pretty, slightly doll-like as usual. A little sugar boy.

Vexed by my silence, he urged me:

'Well, come along, out with it!'

'Out with what?'

'Was it fun, last night? What did *somebody* say to explain my not being there?'

I loosed my tongue with an effort:

'He told me you were wearing an impossible tie.'

How stupid he was, this boy! Couldn't he see the miracle, then? I should have thought it was blindingly obvious. However, I was not in the least hurry to enlighten him. He burst into a shrill laugh: I winced.

'Ha, ha! . . . an impossible tie! Yes, the whole truth is contained in those three words. What do you think of the story? You know my *crêpe-de-Chine* cravat, don't you? It was Charlie, who gave it me!'

'I think,' I said in all sincerity, 'that you were quite right not to change it. I think that cravat's exquisite.'

'Isn't it? A charming idea, that drapery pinned with pearls! I knew I could trust your taste, Claudinette. However,' he added with a polite smile, 'it didn't prevent my amiable father from depriving me of that evening with you. I would have brought you home. I was already looking forward to that delicious little moment in the cab . . .'

Where, oh where had his eyes been all this time? It was

positively pitiful, such blindness! He must have heard some wounding things yesterday night, for, at the thought of them, his face had hardened and his mouth become thin.

'Tell me all about it, Claudine. My dear father was exquisite and witty as usual? He didn't treat you, as he did me, as a "filthy little beast" and a "child with revolting habits"? God,' he fumed, firing up with resentment, 'what a swine, what a . . .'

'No!'

I had interrupted with a violence that had brought me to my feet, face to face with him.

Without moving a muscle, he stared at me, turned pale, grasped what I meant, and stood up too. There was a silence in which I could hear Fanchette's purring, the tick-tock of my little watch, Marcel's breathing, and the pounding of my heart. A silence that lasted, perhaps, two whole minutes . . .

'You too?' he said, at last, in a cynical voice. 'I thought Papa didn't go in for young girls. Usually he's all for married women or tarts.'

I said nothing: I was past speaking.

'And . . . this is quite recent? Only since last night, perhaps? Thank me, Claudine. After all, you owe this marvellous piece of luck to my cravat.'

His delicate, pinched nose was as white as his teeth. I still said nothing; something prevented me.

Standing behind the chair that separated us, he sneered at me. With my hands hanging and my head lowered, I looked up at him; the lace of my little apron fluttered with the beating of my heart. The silence fell once more; interminable. Suddenly, he began to speak again, in a peculiar voice:

'I've always thought you very intelligent, Claudine. And what you're doing at this moment increases my respect for your . . . shrewdness.'

Stupefied, I lifted my head.

'I repeat, you're a remarkable girl, Claudine. And I congratulate you, unreservedly, a nice piece of work.'

I did not understand. But I quietly moved away the chair that separated us. I had a vague notion that, in a moment or two, it would be in my way.

156

'Come, come now, you know perfectly well what I mean. After all, though he's got through quite a bit of money, Papa's still well worth your powder and shot.'

Quicker than a wasp, I flung all my nails at his face; for the last minute I had been taking aim at his eyes. With a shrill scream, he staggered over backwards, his hands up to his face, then, recovering his balance, he rushed to the glass over the chimneypiece. The lower eyelid was torn and bleeding, a little blood was already staining the lapel of his jacket. In a state of crazy exaltation I could hear myself giving little muffled, involuntary shrieks. He turned round, quite beside himself: I thought he wanted to seize a weapon and I rummaged feverishly in my work-bag. My scissors, my scissors! But he wasn't even thinking of hitting me, pushing me aside, he rushed to the jug and dipped his handkerchief in the water. He was already bending over my basin – what impudence! I was on him in a flash, I grabbed his bent head by its two ears and I pushed him back into the room, screaming at him in a hoarse voice I did not recognize:

'No, no, not here! Run away and get your wounds dressed at Charlie's!'

With his handkerchief over his eye, he picked up his hat and went out, forgetting his gloves. I opened all the doors for him and I listened to his footsteps tottering down the stairs. Then I went back into my bedroom and I stood there, I don't know for how long, thinking of nothing at all. At last the limpness of my legs forced me to sit down. This movement started up my thinking mechanism again, and I collapsed. Money! Money! He had dared to say that I wanted money! All the same, that was a fine claw-stroke I'd given him – that little piece of skin that hung down – I swear I only missed the eye by less than a centimetre. The coward, he ought to have bashed me on the head! Ugh, the little milksop, mopping himself up. Money! Money! Whatever should I do with it? I'd more than enough for Fanchette and me. Oh, dear Renaud, I'd tell him everything, and I'd nestle close against him, and he would be so kind and sweet that it would make me cry.

That boy I'd scratched – he'd been eaten up with jealousy; disgusting little *girl* of a boy!

Suddenly I understood, and my temples throbbed painfully. It was *his* money, Marcel's money, I should take if I became Renaud's wife; it was *his* money he was trembling for! And how could I prevent that unfeeling boy from believing in Claudine's cupidity? He would not be the only one to believe in it and he'd tell, they'd all tell Renaud that the girl was selling herself, that she'd inveigled the poor man who was going through the dangerous forties. What could I do? What could I do? I wanted to see Renaud, I didn't want Marcel's money, but I wanted Renaud all the same. Suppose I asked Papa for help? Oh, dear – my head ached so dreadfully – oh, my dear, sweet place on his shoulder, must I give up? No! Rather than that, I'd blow up everything! I'd tie that Marcel up here in my bedroom, and I'd kill him. And afterwards I'd tell the police he'd tried to seduce me and I'd killed him in self-defence. *There*!

Right up to the time when Fanchette woke me up by mewing that she was hungry, I remained huddled up in the tub-chair, with one finger on each eye and one finger in each ear, overwhelmed with wild dreams, black despair . . . and love.

'Dinner? No, I don't want any dinner. I've got a migraine. Make me some fresh lemonade, Mélie, I'm dying of thirst. I'm going to bed.' Papa and Mélie, anxious and disturbed, hovered round my bed till nine o'clock. At last, I could stand it no more and implored them: 'Oh, do go away – I'm so tired.'

As I lay in the dark, I could hear the servants down in the courtyard banging doors and washing dishes. I desperately needed Renaud! Why hadn't I sent him a telegram straight away? Now it was too late. Tomorrow would never come. My friend, my dear life, the man to whom I would trust myself as to a beloved father, the man with whom I felt alternately ashamed and apprehensive, as if I were his mistress – then happy and uninhibited as if he rocked me in his arms when I was little.

After hours of fever, of painful throbbing in my head, of silent appeals to someone who was too far away and did not hear, my demented thoughts began to clear a little. Towards three in the morning, they gradually shifted back, leaving an empty space in which, at last, there appeared the Idea. It came with the dawn, the Idea, with the awakening of the sparrows and the fleeting coolness that precedes a summer day. Thunderstruck by it, I lay perfectly still on my back in bed, with my eyes wide open. How simple it was and how I had tortured myself for nothing! Now I should have circles round my eyes and drawn cheeks when Renaud came. And the solution had been staring me in the face all the time! I didn't want Marcel to think: 'Claudine's got her eye on my money.' I didn't want to say to Renaud: 'Go away and don't love me any more.' Oh God, that was the last thing I wanted to say to him! But I didn't want to be his wife either, and, to soothe *my* irritable conscience – very well, then, I'd be his mistress!

Revived and refreshed, I went to sleep. I slept like a sack, flat on my stomach, with my face hidden in my folded arms. The declamatory voice of my classic old beggar awoke me. I felt completely relaxed, but startled. Ten o'clock already! 'Mélie, throw the old man four sous!'

Mélie did not hear. I slipped on my dressing-gown, and ran into the drawing-room barefooted, with my hair standing wildly on end. 'Old man, here's ten sous. Keep the change!' What a beautiful white beard! No doubt he possesses a country house and an estate, like most of the beggars in Paris. So much the better for him. And, as I was going back to my room, I ran into Monsieur Maria who had just arrived, and who stood still, dazzled by my morning déshabille.

'Monsieur Maria, don't you think that today's going to be the end of the world?'

'Alas, no, Mademoiselle.'

'*I* think it is. You just see.'

Sitting in my tub of warm water, I studied myself lingeringly and minutely. That down, surely that didn't count as hair on my legs? Bother, my nipples weren't as pink as Luce's but my legs were longer and more elegant, and I had dimples in my back. I wasn't a Rubens, far from it, but I'm not keen on the 'beautiful butcher's wife' type – neither is Renaud.

Renaud – that name spoken almost aloud when I was dressed in nothing but a beechwood tub – intimidated me a good deal. Eleven o'clock. Still five hours to wait. All was going well. I brushed and brushed my curls, I brushed my teeth, I brushed my nails! Everything must shine, shine, shine! Filmy stockings, a new chemise, knickers to match, my pink corsets, my finely-striped silk petticoat that goes *frou frou* when I move.

Gay as I used to be at School, active and bustling, I busied myself with anything and everything to stop myself from thinking what might be going to happen. After all, if it was today I was going to offer myself, he might very well take me today if he wanted to – it was entirely up to him. But oh, I hoped he wouldn't want me quite so quickly, quite so suddenly – it wouldn't be in the least like him. I counted on him, yes, far more on him than on myself. For, as they say in Montigny, I'd completely lost my 'rudder'.

SIXTEEN

THE AFTERNOON WAS hard to get through, all the same. He might not come to see me. At three o'clock I began to play at being a panther in a cage and my ears were stretched to their utmost. At twenty to four, there was a faint ring at the bell. But I was deceived; it was definitely he. Standing with my back against the foot of the bed, I ceased to exist. The door opened and closed behind Renaud. He was bareheaded; he seemed to have grown a little thinner. His moustached trembled imperceptibly and his eyes gleamed blue in the dimness. I did not move; I did not speak. He was taller. He was paler. His face was shadowed, tired, arrogant. Still standing by the door, without advancing into the room, he spoke very low.

'Good afternoon, Claudine.'

Drawn to him by the sound of his voice, I went to him and held out my two hands. He kissed them both, but he let them drop again.

'Are you angry with me, little friend?'

I gave an ineffable shrug. I sat down in the armchair. He sat down on the low chair and I quickly went up close to him, ready to throw myself into his arms. Hateful man! He did not seem to understand. He spoke almost under his breath, as if he were frightened:

'My sweet, crazy child, you said a thousand things to me yesterday that sleep and daylight have driven right out of your mind. Wait a minute, don't look at me too much with those adorable eyes, Claudine! Eyes I shall never forget that were too kind to me. All last night and the rest of that other night, I've been fighting against a mad, ridiculous hope. I'd ceased to be aware that I was forty,' he went on with effort, 'but I realized you would remember the fact, if not today or tomorrow, at any rate very soon. My darling with the too-loving eyes, my little curly shepherd,' he said, even lower for there was a lump in his throat and his eyes were wet, 'don't tempt me any more. I'm nothing but a poor dazzled man, utterly swept away by you. Defend yourself, Claudine! My God, it's monstrous; in other people's eyes, you might be my daughter!'

'But I am your daughter too!' (I held out my arms to him.) 'Don't you *feel* that I'm your daughter? I was that from the very beginning – ever since those very first days – I've been your obedient, astonished child. And much, much more astonished a little later on to feel that so many things were coming to her all at once – a father, a friend, a master, a lover. Oh, don't say no, don't stop me, let me say a lover too! A lover – one can find that any day – but someone who's every-thing all at the same time – someone, who, if he goes away, leaves you a widow and an orphan, and utterly friendless – isn't that an incredible miracle? *You're* that miracle! I adore you!'

He lowered his eyes, but too late. A tear trickled down on to his moustache. Desperate, I flung my arms round his neck.

'Are you unhappy? Have I hurt you without meaning to?'

The great arms I was waiting for closed tight round me at last; the blue-black eyes told me what I wanted to know.

'Oh my girl, my girl beyond all hope! Don't give me time to be ashamed of what I'm doing! I'm keeping you, I can't do anything but keep you . . . your little body is the loveliest thing to me in the whole world. Shall I ever be completely old if I have you? My darling, my bird, if you only knew how possessive my love is, how boyishly jealous. And what an intolerable husband I shall be!'

A husband? Why, of course, he didn't know! I came to, tore myself away from my dear place, after one furtive kiss, and brusquely untwined my arms.

'No, not my husband.'

He stared at me, his eyes intoxicated and tender, and kept his arms open.

'It's very serious. I ought to have told you at once. But . . . you upset all my resolutions when I saw you come in. And then I'd waited for you so long, I just couldn't say a word. Sit down there. Don't hold my waist . . . nor my arm . . . nor my hand . . . please! It would be almost better not to look at me, Renaud.'

Seated in the little tub-chair, I put out my arms and thrust away his eager hands with all the resolution I had left. He sat down, very, very close, on the Breton chair.

'Marcel came here yesterday afternoon. Yes. He asked me to tell him all about the night before last . . . as if it *could* be told, Renaud! And he congratulated me on my artfulness! Apparently, you're still quite rich, and, by becoming your wife, it's his fortune, Marcel's, I should be pinching for my own advantage.'

Renaud had leapt to his feet. His nostrils were quivering in the most menacing way; I hastily ended my speech.

'So, I don't want to marry you . . .'

The shuddering sigh I heard urged me on to finish.

'. . . but I *do* want to be your mistress.'

'Oh! Claudine!'

'What do you mean, Claudine?'

He considered me, with his arms dropped and his eyes full of such admiration and such distress that I no longer knew what to think. I had been expecting a triumph, a wild embrace, perhaps almost too eager acquiescence.

'Don't you think it's a good idea? Do you imagine I'd ever let people think that I don't love you better than anything in the world? *I've* got money, too. I've got a hundred and fifty thousand francs. *There*, what do you say to that? I don't need Marcel's money.'

'Claudine!'

'I'd better own up to everything,' I said, looking up to him coaxingly. 'I scratched him – Marcel, I mean. I . . . I tore off a little bit of his cheek and I threw him out of the flat.'

The remembrance made me stand up and begin to act the scene for him and my amazon-like gestures forced him to

163

smile under his moustache. But what was he waiting for? Why didn't he accept my offer at once? Hadn't he understood, then?

'So ... so you see,' I said in a voice that was becoming rather embarrassed, 'I want to be your mistress. It won't be difficult, you know how much freedom, I'm allowed. Well, I give you all that freedom, I'd like to give you my whole life. But you have to go away on business quite a lot. When you're free, you can come here, and I'll come to your flat, too – your famous flat! You won't think your home's too much like an eighteenth-century engraving any more, will you? Not for a Claudine who completely belongs to you?'

My legs were shaking a little, so I sat down again. He sank down on his knees, with his face on a level with mine; he stopped me talking by laying his mouth on mine for barely a second, without any pressure. He drew it back, alas, at the moment when the kiss was beginning to make my head whirl. With his arms round me, he talked to me in a voice he could not quite control.

'Oh, Claudine! Little girl, who's got all her knowledge out of nasty books, is there anything in the world as pure as you are? No, my darling, my delight, I'm not going to let you get away with this lunatic generosity! If I take you, it's for good, for ever and ever. And, in front of everyone, in the ordinary, decent, conventional way, I shall marry you.'

'No, you won't marry me!'

I needed courage, for, when he called me 'my darling', 'my delight', all my blood drained away and my bones turned soft.

'I'll be your mistress, or nothing.'

'My wife, or nothing!'

Suddenly struck by the strangeness of this debate, I broke into a nervous laugh. As I was laughing, with my mouth open and my head thrown back, I saw him leaning over me, so tortured with desire that I trembled, then, bravely, I opened my arms, thinking he was accepting me.

But he shook his head and said, in a choked voice:

'No!'

What could I do? I clasped my hands; I implored; I offered him my mouth, my eyes half-closed. He repeated again, almost as if he were being strangled:

'No! My wife or nothing.'

Slowly, I stood up, feeling utterly helpless and lost.

During those few seconds Renaud, as if suddenly inspired, had reached the drawing-room door. He already had his hand on the study-door when I guessed. The wretch! He was going to ask Papa for my hand!

Without daring to scream, I hung on to his arm, imploring him under my breath:

'Oh, if you love me, don't do it! Mercy, anything you like. Do you want Claudine this very minute? Don't ask Papa anything, wait a few days. Do you think . . . it's revolting, this money business! Marcel's venomous. He'll tell everyone, he'll say I seduced you by force. I love you, I love you . . .'

He took me in his arms, the coward, and kissed me slowly on my cheeks, on my eyes, on my hair, under the ear just where it makes you shudder. What could I do, in his arms?

And, noiselessly he opened the door, as he gave me one final kiss. I had only just time to break away quickly.

Papa, sitting cross-legged on the floor among his papers, his beard dishevelled and his nose pugnacious, glared at us ferociously. We had chosen a bad moment.

'What the devil are you doing, butting in here? Ah, it's you, my dear Sir, I'm delighted to see you!'

Renaud recovered a little of his self-possession and formality, though bereft of hat and gloves.

'The fact is, Sir, I should like to have a minute's serious conversation with you.'

'Impossible,' said Papa categorically. 'Absolutely impossible before tomorrow. This,' he explained, pointing to Monsieur Maria who was writing – writing too fast – 'this is of the utmost urgency.'

'But, Sir, what *I* want to say to you is of the utmost urgency.'

'Say it straight out then.'

'I want – I implore you, try not to think me too outrageously absurd – I want to marry Claudine.'

'Is that business going to start again?' thundered Papa, who had leapt to his feet and looked really formidable. 'God's thunder, ten thousand herds of sacred swine, all sons of bitches! But don't you realize this she-donkey doesn't want to get married? She'll tell you so herself, that she doesn't love you!'

Under the storm, Renaud regained all his swagger. He waited for the oaths to come to an end, then, looking down at me quizzically under his drooping lashes, he said:

'She doesn't love me? Claudine, do you dare to say you don't love me?'

Goodness me, no, I didn't dare. And, with all my heart, I murmured:

'Yes, of course I love you.'

Papa, dumbfounded, contemplated his daughter as if she were a slug that had fallen from Mars.

'Well, this is staggering? And you, do you love her?'

'Definitely,' said Renaud, nodding his head.

'Extraordinary!' marvelled Papa, with sublime unconsciousness. 'Oh, I'm perfectly willing! But personally, when it comes to marrying, she wouldn't be at all my type. I prefer women more . . .'

And his hands sketched the outline of the breasts of a nursing mother. What could I say? I was beaten. Renaud had cheated. I whispered to him very softly standing on tiptoe to reach his ear:

'You know, I don't want Marcel's money.'

His face young and radiant under his silver hair, he pulled me into the drawing-room, as he replied, lightly and spitefully:

'Pooh! He'll still have all his grandmother's to batten on!'

And the two of us went back to my room, his arms tight round me, carrying me off as if he were stealing me; both of us as ecstatic and silly as the lovers of romance.